MURDER
ON THE
BOULEVARD

For Bob & Nita —
my fellow writer
& friend —

ANNE SLOAN

Anne Sloan

June 18, 1996

HOUSTON, TEXAS
1996

ISBN 0-942031-00-8

Book production & design by
Portier Gorman, Inc.
Thibodaux, Louisiana

ACKNOWLEDGEMENTS

Beginning with my introduction to Sister Agatha's book, *The History of Houston Heights*, I fell in love with the town. I have tried to recreate the social history, recorded in the newspapers and magazines of this period. My book is a novel. Although it refers to actual historical figures and events which occurred in Houston and the Heights, the circumstances surrounding them are fictional.

I thank the librarians at the Central Public Library and Houston Heights Branch who helped me with my research and Rangers at the Big Thicket National Preserve who helped me with the topography and history of their park. Readers of the manuscript providing invaluable suggestions and encouragement were Nita Armstrong, Patricia Brison, Celeste Byrom, Betty Chapman, Elizabeth Donnelly, Jim Gedeon, Nancy Krpec, and especially Nancy Tucker, Gail Glass, and Kendra Williams who were with me chapter by chapter. Seymour Sacks and Richard K. Ragland are two gentlemen whose reminiscences are threaded throughout this book.

THIS BOOK IS
DEDICATED TO

THE HOUSTON HEIGHTS
ASSOCIATION

PROCEEDS FROM
THE SALE OF THIS BOOK
WILL BENEFIT THE HOUSTON HEIGHTS
ASSOCIATION AND ITS MANY EFFORTS
TO PRESERVE THE HERITAGE
AND HISTORY OF
HOUSTON HEIGHTS.

PROLOGUE

HOUSTON HEIGHTS
August 1912

The man stumbled out of the building and staggered toward the esplanade, crossing the Boulevard and continuing until he reached the trolley stop. He rubbed the brim of his bowler and lowered his trembling fingers. His shoulders prickled. The confrontation had upset him more than he thought it would. He pulled a handkerchief from his coat pocket and mopped the sweat from his brow. What time did the streetcars run after dark? He couldn't remember. Looking down the wide, handsome boulevard, he thought of the fairyland O.M. Carter had created here, and his lips curved into a weak smile.

The clanging of Trolley Car 206 interrupted his thoughts. Intent upon flagging the driver to stop, he failed to notice the figure which stood waiting behind him. When the trolley was a block away, too far for the motorman to see him waving in the dusky twilight, he felt a hard thwack and fell forward, grabbing the night air. His head hit the wooden tracks. He never saw the trolley nor felt the wheels pass over him.

CHAPTER ONE
BIG THICKET, MAY 1908

H oly thunderation!" she exclaimed. "He's gone to Houston without me. Fool! I should've hired my own rig, and I should never have come without Dessie." As she damned her ill-fortune, a crow circling overhead seemed to mock her with its raucous cries, and she shook her fist at it before turning back to stare down the sandy country lane.

Taking off her sweat-stained duster, she glanced at the lapel watch pinned to her shirtwaist. A mournful whistle announced the afternoon train to Houston was on its way.

Flora Logan had not reckoned with this. If her father found out about her trip, he would pitch a running fit. "He'll really have something to be mad about." She strode down the lane, wondering why she was surprised at being stranded. Wasn't this her special talent? Getting into trouble. She tossed her head and announced to the cloud-strewn sky, "I don't care if I do!"

She meant for the day to be a grand adventure. The Big Thicket with its carnivorous pitcher plants and wild orchids was the field trip of a lifetime. The motivation of her friend Dessie to tag along had been less grandiose. "You can't go out there alone," she'd said. "It wouldn't be proper."

The trip's planning had been one of great delicacy. Her father would not have understood the importance of this outing, much less have given his permission. She had crossed her fingers the evening he announced he was going to Belville to deliver a pink granite lamb he had carved as a gravestone for a five year old girl, dead of diphtheria. When her mother decided to accompany him, Flora began to make her plans. Going by wagon, the trip would take her parents two days, enough time for her to get to the Big Thicket and back.

She had left home right after her parents' departure. Unfortunately, while she was pedalling her bicycle down the shell surfaced Boulevard, Mr. Murphy's milk wagon rumbled alongside. She was sure her large straw hat hid her red braids. Hunching her shoulders, she hoped her oversized smock covered the

1

daring split skirt she was wearing. Surely, he wouldn't recognize her in the gray light of dawn.

Her bubble of hope burst though as she heard, "Hallo, Flora Logan, what you doing riding your bicycle at daybreak? The sun's not even up." Mr. Murphy's voice boomed at her as he passed by.

She waved and pointed toward the wooden bridge that crossed White Oak Bayou, "Going fishing."

He yelled over his shoulder, "Where's your pole?"
Then he laughed and added, "Watch yourself, Missy."

He had probably recognized her bicycle. She shouldn't have made Nellie so distinctive, but she couldn't resist painting a rich hunter green over the dull black metal and outlining the tire covers in a snappy metallic gold. Of all people to see her. Mr. Murphy would tell everyone in town she had been riding her bicycle alone at dawn.

The three story orphanage where Dessie lived with her Aunt Ferdie came into view just after she turned onto Washington, and she wheeled in beside the porch and easily lifted her bicycle up the stairs. She had met Dessie Trichelle her first day at Harvard Elementary School.

Five or six girls had been playing jumprope as Flora walked out to the dirt playground for recess. She stood back, slumping as usual, so she wouldn't look so tall, chewed on one of her long red braids, and watched the group. Dessie was the jumper, small and nimble, her blond sausage curls bouncing around her soft pink cheeks, her blue and white dotted pinafore, still crisp and clean. Suddenly, the blonde angel looked over at the bedraggled redhead, slouching against the tallow tree, her middy blouse and skirt wrinkled and stained, her navy stockings twisted around her thin legs. She lifted her arm and beckoned Flora to jump in. Looking around to see who this girl might be inviting, Flora turned red as a beet when she realized it was she. Grinning, she went over and took her place with the blonde, and the rope-thrower adeptly threw the rope higher and wider to accommodate Dessie's larger playmate. The two girls jumped in unison facing each other and giggling. They kept it up until the thrower started "hot pepper," and Dessie misstepped, and they lost their turn. Breathlessly, the two girls introduced themselves,

Dessie announcing that she was an orphan, Flora that she was an only child. As if by magic, they became friends. Over the years residents of the Heights shook their heads in wonder at the comradeship of the girls, who were so different yet so devoted to one another. When Dessie's Aunt Ferdie had founded this home for the orphaned boys she had seen selling papers on Houston streets, she and Dessie worked hard to keep it running smoothly. Flora was frequently there lending a hand.

Flora banged the screened door open and bounded up the bare wooden stairs to the second floor, knowing that the "newsies" would have long since headed to Franklin Street to get their bundles of *The Houston Post.*

As soon as she entered Dessie's bedroom, she could see her friend would not be going with her today. With a sinking heart, she watched as the petite blonde ran to the chamber pot and was sick. Flora went to the blue graniteware pitcher and poured water from it into the washbowl, then dampened the frayed linen towel, and handed it to her. Turning back to the washstand, she picked up a small bottle, removed the stopper and poured cucumber astringent on a handkerchief and patted Dessie's brow. She splashed some on her own face as she said, "There, I feel better, but obviously you don't." She glanced at Dessie's ashen face, her china blue eyes ringed with dark circles, and reminded herself that Dessie had always had a weak stomach. "You know how sick those peanuts always make you when we go to the baseball games."

"I'm sorry, Flora, I've ruined your expedition, but I can't get on a train the way I feel. I know how much this trip meant to you. Please forgive me?"

"Oh, Dessie, don't be a goose. I understand! It's probably those oysters you ate last night, or maybe the excitement at dining at the Brazos Hotel for the first time." Flora paused and then continued nonchalantly, "Since everything is planned, I'll go on by myself." This out, she steeled herself for what she knew her friend would say.

"Flora Logan, that's the stupidest idea I've ever heard."

"Well, that may be, but I've made up my mind; I'm going through with it alone." Flora spoke with a conviction she did not quite feel. "My knapsack is packed with my journal and pencils;

3

I've got crackers, two tins of sardines. . ." She nervously smoothed the pink and blue quilt which lay at the foot of Dessie's bed as she listened to her friend's warnings.

"If your Mama and Papa ever hear about this?. . . It scares me just to think about it. Have you forgotten your father's reaction to your swim in Rocky Bottom? He just got over being up in the air because you skipped church last month and went with that group on a cotton barge down to the San Jacinto Battlegrounds."

"I know. Swimming holes shouldn't be for boys only. I'm as good a swimmer as any of them. Besides, I was better covered than they were. I wore bloomers."

"I'm glad he never found out I made the bloomers. He would have come after me with that same strap. You and your papa have more in common than your red hair. You inherited your stubbornness from him too."

"Maybe so, but he's got to realize I'm old enough to make my own decisions." Flora dropped the edge of the quilt and patted Dessie's arm. "I'm going on as we planned--the first train to Beaumont, then I'll hire a rig to drive out to the edge of the woods. Once I'm there, I'll do what we set out to do and nothing more."

Because she knew it was futile to argue, Dessie answered only in words of caution. "Be careful, Flora, and promise me you won't go deep into the Thicket. They say people get lost in there and are never seen again."

"When I get off the train tonight, I'll stop by and tell you all about my trip. Maybe I'll even spend the night." Flora picked up her battered valise, and blew Dessie a kiss.

As she went downstairs, Annie called from the kitchen. Flora entered and saw her pulling shallow, round pans out of the oven. The sweet, yeasty aroma of cinnamon buns filled the room. Setting the pans on the counter, the kindly old cook wiped her sweaty hands on her pink gingham apron and looked anxiously behind Flora for Dessie.

"I thought I heard Miss Dessie up last night. She ate them dad-blamed oysters, didn't she? I tell her agin and agin,'Gal, don't you go eatin' in them highfalutin' cookhouses. Your weak stomach can't do with all that fancied-up food,' but she goes

4

and does it anyways."

"She'll be fine with a day's rest; just look in on her and make her some creamed toast, something gentle for her stomach."

"I knows how to take care of Miss Dessie, don't you think I don't." She narrowed her eyes as she took in Flora's costume. "And where're you goin' at this time of the mornin', half-dressed in that funny looking skirt and totin' that beat up old satchel?"

Flora looked at the blue chambray split skirt that grazed the toes of her boots and wondered if being fashionably daring was worth the criticism that accompanied it. She studied the floor and then with a shrug announced, "I'm taking the early train to Beaumont and coming back by dinner. Dessie was supposed to come with me; but, of course, now she can't."

"You're gonna do what? Mercy me, what you lost in East Texas? Ain't nothin' would get me back in the middle of those piney woods." Her face became a thundercloud. "Your mamma and papa know what you're up to? Naw, I didn't think so. Well, you always done just what you like anyways." Annie added her own words of caution. "Let me tell you there's some bad characters over there that come for this here Spindletop oil stuff and never left. You'd better watch your step, young lady. You apt to get more'n you planned for." Annie grumbled, and then, having spoken her mind, asked, "Don't you want me to pack you a bite to eat? You eat that train food, Miss Flora, and you'll be in the same shape as Miss Dessie, you hear?" Like Dessie, Annie seemed to know it was hopeless to argue with this headstrong girl. She lowered her voice and muttered under her breath as she shuffled back to the stove, "I wish you'd eaten those oysters too, so you wouldn't be traipsin' off like this."

"Annie, I've packed some food, but could I have one of those buns and a cup of coffee before I go?"

"You sure can." She filled a pottery mug with hot coffee, went to the icebox and removed one of the bottles of milk Mr. Murphy had left on the back porch before daylight, skimmed off the cream into a bowl, and poured the milk into an ironstone cereal pitcher.

Flora grabbed a bun from the pan and settled on the long bench in front of the scarred pine table that took up most of the kitchen. She stirred a spoonful of sugar into the steaming mug of coffee and poured in the fresh milk.

Picking up a copy of *The Post*, she scanned the headlines. "It's a red-letter day for Houston, Annie." The cook turned from the drainboard and gave her a questioning look. "The city's taking over operation of the new ship channel; guess anyone could've expected that. The army engineers finished, but it's only eighteen-and-a-half feet, and apparently that's not deep enough." Flora could see she'd lost Annie's attention, and she muttered to herself, "I bet the people of Houston will be asked to pay to make it deeper! That's another reason, my father would say, for living in Houston Heights."

"Miss Flora, whatcha' talkin' about? Who's ever heard of a young lady talkin' about ship channels, army engineers, and stuff like that. You need to think on gettin' youself a husband, not worryin' your pretty head about bi'ness. I bet Miss Dessie won't have no trouble along that line. I never see her down here studyin' anything but the society pages. She reads me about all them parties, interestin' things that happen right here in the Heights, and sometimes she even reads me the serials. Why, one time, there was this lady that lived someplace foreign, lemme see. . ."

Flora jumped up at the break in Annie's thoughts, crammed the last bite of roll in her mouth and washed it down with a large gulp of coffee, "Sorry, Annie, gotta run. Thanks for the breakfast. When you check on Dessie, give her some extra care for me." Flora hugged the ample waist of the orphanage's favorite employee, grabbed her satchel, and lifted her duster off the hook behind the door.

She sat her case down when she reached the entry hall, slid into her washed-out gray cotton coat, snagged her straw hat from the hall tree, and slammed it on her head as she headed out the front door. Annie stood in the doorway and watched her leave, calling out, "Be careful, Miss Flora." Then muttering to herself, "That gal's just like a colt, all long legs and wildness. Some man's gonna have a job on his hands trying to tame her."

Flora walked the few blocks down Washington Avenue to Grand Central Station. Entering the depot, she went up to the counter and purchased a round-trip ticket to Beaumont as if she did it every day. The man at the ticket counter raised his eyebrows and gave her a funny look. She noticed there was only one other unaccompanied lady in the station. A man shouted "all aboard," and she hurried to the tracks. The porter helped her board the single passenger car which would be making the trip.

Flora collapsed on the stiff seat, and looked around. She'd been on a train only one other time, a trip with her dad to look at some granite near Austin. Dissatisfied with the quality of stone being shipped for the markers and monuments he manufactured, he'd gone north to look at the sources. The train car they had ridden was like a palace, red velvet seats with bouncy springs and curtains on the windows. This car wasn't so nice, but as long as it got her there, she didn't care.

Flora knew her dad to be a gifted stonemason who could have done better in the East where fine marble decorations were commonplace, but ten years ago he'd chosen to move down from New York and settle in Houston Heights. He told his family that he had chosen the new planned community because it provided country living and was built on an elevated site that would be free of yellow fever epidemics. She felt he was more impressed by the rail service provided and the streetcar system that facilitated the three mile trip to Houston.

It had been a good move for the family. Fred Logan had prospered, and Flora had made friends in the new town. Several years ago her parents had taken in Caleb, an orphaned cousin of her mother's. He was two years her junior and seemed younger, but if she'd known Dessie wasn't coming, she would have asked him along. As the train's clicket-clacking carried her along, she began to wish for him. She hoped her father would adopt him and train him to take over the marble business. Having only a daughter had been a disappointment for Fred Logan, and she knew she'd been a disappointment in other ways, too.

She removed her dark blue leather journal from her satchel and smoothed the cover of this graduation gift from her biology teacher at Heights High. When Flora entered high school her self-taught knowledge of botany almost equaled that of her teacher's, and by her senior year, she was conducting field trips for students in the woods north of the Heights. Ever since she had read an account of the Big Thicket located northeast of Houston, she had dreamed of going there. Dessie had been reluctant, but Flora vividly described the beautiful wild orchids they were sure to see, and she had finally consented. Flora knew that Dessie's illness was not feigned, but it had occurred conveniently for someone who was not enthusiastic about going.

Now that she was on the train headed for Beaumont at a dizzying speed, Flora wondered how she would get from the depot to her destination. She had lightheartedly told Dessie she would hire a rig, but she'd never done so before, and knew she would be at a disadvantage in a livery stable. She was also uncertain how far it was to the edge of the Thicket. According to her map, it seemed to sprawl over the entire area. Straightening her shoulders, she told herself that she would know it when she saw it.

She took off her duster, raised the train window and looked out at endless fields of cotton plants. The melodic notes of the train's whistle filled the countryside. Ditches along the tracks were filled with primroses blooming among patch after patch of mullein. In ancient times, mullein's grey hairy branches had been dried and dipped in fat for use as torches. "Hag's Taper," it had been called, because people believed witches used it as light for their ceremonies. Nowadays, she knew people looked at it and saw a scruffy weed.

The conductor came by to punch her ticket, and as she handed it to him she recognized the passenger sitting two rows behind her, a salesmen who called on her father at the marble yard. Fred Logan had brought him home for dinner a few times. She had secretly laughed at this pompous man who was so proud of his satin waistcoats. Hatless, his thinning brown hair was parted in the middle with fluffy curls fringing his over-sized ears. Mindful of her need for assistance, she called to him as if he were a long lost friend. "Hello, Mr. Fain, remember me, Flora, Fred Logan's daughter? Are you going to Beaumont too?"

Ward Fain squinted in her direction and continued polishing his spectacles with a large white handkerchief. He replaced them on his nose and looked at her in surprise. "Yes, I am, Miss Logan, and what brings you up here today?"

Flora stood and made her way to his row. "I'm going on a botanical field trip to gather specimens in the Big Thicket." She spoke animatedly to arouse his interest in her trip. His reaction was not what she expected.

"Young lady, you're one crazy redhead, aren't you? No, I'm sorry; I shouldn't have said that. I apologize for thinking you intend to go into the Thicket by yourself. You're meeting some other students?"

"Well, I was supposed to have a partner, but she became ill and couldn't come. I don't suppose you're renting a buggy when you get to Beaumont?"

"How else would I go around to the stores and sell hard-ware? By bicycle?" He snickered impolitely.

Flora thought of the consequences if she failed to win over this odious man and gritted her teeth. "Mr. Fain," she said brightly, "if I paid part of the cost of the rig, would you take me to the edge of the Big Thicket? I'm not going deep into the woods. I want to observe some of the different plants, trees and shrubs. Could you leave me there and pick me up when you get through calling on your customers?"

"How about the snakes and bobcats and panthers? Are you going to record seeing those too? Or will you just ignore them?" Ward asked with a sneer.

She ignored his remark, visions of wild orchids in her head and tried smiling coyly, "Please, Mr. Fain, it would be so helpful if I didn't have to go to the livery stable alone."

Ward Fain frowned, and Flora noticed for the first time how weak-chinned he was. She spent the next half hour trying to convince him that this trip was an important part of her re-search project and might help her get a scholarship to Hunts-ville Normal College. She knew she had won when he finally looked at her with a silly grin.

"Beaumont, next stop," the conductor yelled. Flora was relieved that her last obstacle had been overcome. Mr. Fain led her to the livery stable where he hired a serviceable looking cart and hollow-backed grey gelding, loaded his sample cases in the bed of the wagon, and motioned Flora to climb aboard. Clutch-ing her satchel with one hand and her straw hat with the other, she set out with Ward Fain down the dusty country lane toward

Lumberton.

In less than two hours, they reached what appeared to be the outer edges of the Thicket. Fain had entertained her along the way with descriptions of the black panther's cries. "It sounds like a woman screaming for help. I only heard it once, but I'll never forget it. A fellow in Silsbee swears a panther followed him down this very road almost to Beaumont." He grinned slyly as he stopped the buggy so that Flora could hop down.

"I appreciate the warning, Mr. Fain; but I'll be fine." She set off toward the woods after they settled on three o'clock as the time for him to come back. "Thank you, so much, sir, I'll never forget this kindness." Later, Flora was to wince when she recalled these words.

She scarcely heard the rattling of the rig as he drove away. With her first step into the nearby grove of towering Beech trees, she entered another world. Wide-eyed and open-mouthed, she stared at the largest Southern Magnolia she'd ever seen. "Those branches must be more than thirty feet long."

She smelled her first baygall before she saw it. She had read that these sloughs were created when open water was cut off from a nearby stream. The fetid black water was silent and murky, lit only by occasional patches of sunlight heavily filtered by the thick canopy of trees. A striped salamander sunned itself on a fallen stump and a cotton-mouth moccasin did the same on a flat rock at the water's edge. Recalling Mr. Fain's words about panthers and bobcats, she shrugged her shoulders and stepped over a fallen tree.

The silence was broken by a chattering squirrel scolding her from the safety of a longleaf pine's branches. She laughed and called up to the small animal,"Yes, Annie."

Dozens of birds were calling to one another as she walked along the leafy floor of the forest, her boots sinking down into a hundred years of defoliation. Gasping in surprise, she saw a clump of yellow flowers at her feet, bent down, and cupped the delicate wood sorrel, stroking the heart shaped leaves which ancient herbalists had mistakenly used to treat cardiac ailments.

Her eyes continued to study the patches of sunlit ground until she spied what she thought to be a mound of yellow and green trash. Walking closer, she realized it was not refuse, but what she'd come for, the pitcher plants. The drawings in her botany book had not done them justice. These were stiffly upright yellow-green leaves shaped like trumpets, hollow tubes which emitted a honeyed perfume luring insects into its red veined hood. Flora sat back and enjoyed this masterpiece of nature. When she arose to move on, she was surprised that her skirt was dripping wet. She had been sitting in a bog so thickly thatched with meadow grasses that she hadn't even realized it was there.

✂✂✂✂

Ward Fain left Cox's Hardware, glad to make this his last stop for the day. He stowed his sample cases in the buggy tied up in front of the store and walked next door to the saloon. Making his way to the empty counter, he ordered a glass of whiskey, rubbing his hands in satisfaction with the orders he had written up.

Then a clock struck one, and he remembered Flora. What a fool he'd been to let her talk him into being part of her plans. Taking her to the Big Thicket, and worse, leaving her there alone was stupid, but she seemed so determined. He downed his drink and covered his face with his hands, remembering now that Flora Logan was always up to something. She's the one that jumped in the boys' swimming hole; she couldn't go to the Natatorium like all the other young ladies. Always racing up and down the Boulevard on that bicycle of hers. The first time he went to Fred's for supper, Flora scared him to death by greeting him from the top branch of the oak tree in her front yard. Considering that the skirt she was wearing was split like a pair of men's trousers, he didn't think she was much of a lady.

His stomach churned. Her father was a good customer; he would never do business with him again if he knew Ward had helped Flora with her foolhardy plan. Logan probably set great store by this tall fiery-headed wench. Fain's hand shook, and he spilled whiskey on the counter. But what if he didn't go back there? How would she get back? Folks weren't going to believe

11

that he carried her out to the Thicket because she wanted to go. No one would swallow that one, least of all her parents. That mule-headed redhead would come off looking like a pitiful victim, and he'd be skinned alive. Women don't traipse around the countryside by themselves looking for flowers. "Whatever happens to her serves her right . . . No, I better get back there and pick her up right now."

At dusk Fain left the saloon, and staggered toward his rig, bent to untie the reins, and fell to his knees. When he tried to rise, his head grazed the corner of the wagon and he went down again. He lay sprawled beside the back wheel, unnoticed as darkness descended on the small town.

※※※※

Flora emerged from the edge of the Thicket, tired, but radiant. Next time she'd bring more supplies and canvas boots to protect her feet from the muddy swamps, and maybe she'd see the orchids.

Her long straight hair had come loose. She tried replaiting it, but leaves and twigs were caught in the tangled mess that hung down her back. She had discarded her straw hat early on. The shirtwaist had come out of her skirt's waistband as she had gone from plant to plant, bending and stooping to examine each blossom and leaf. She looked down at her mud-crusted boots indifferently.

She sat on the grass near the road where Mr. Fain was to come and opened her satchel, taking out the package of crackers and using her penknife to cut a piece of yellow cheese. It amazed her how few females carried a knife. Wiping her hands on her skirt, she withdrew her journal and pencil and settled herself against a tree trunk, making notes to record what she had seen.

Engrossed in her writing, Flora had no notion of passing time. When she glanced down at her watch and realized it was almost five o'clock, she gasped and jumped to her feet. "What will I do now?" she whispered to no one but the tall grass waving along the side of the road. Picking up her satchel, she started back to town.

12

CHAPTER TWO

S he judged it was nine or ten o'clock when she saw lights and realized she was close to Beaumont. Her lace-up boots had rubbed her feet raw, and she was shaking with exhaustion. As she trudged down the street, she considered her options. Go to the nearest saloon and look for Ward Fain? Look for a hotel but tell them she didn't have enough money to pay for a room? Look for the police station and rely on the officers to get home? Two minutes later the answer became clear.

Flora jumped to one side as a huge, dungaree-clad man came barreling out of the building to her right, landing in the hardened dirt at her feet. Masculine laughter and the tinny music of a cheap piano came from the open doorway. Business was good this evening. The man picked himself up and brushed clouds of dust from his jacket.

Catching sight of her, his bloodshot eyes widened, and he stretched his lips back over bare gums. She returned his once-over appraisal, wheeled around and continued walking.

"Just a minute, Missy, what's your hurry? If you're needing a ride, I got a friend with a rig."

Flora turned to him, her brown eyes snapping. "Thank you, but I need no help from you." He stepped in front of her and grabbed her arms. She turned her head from the stench of his breath and jerked her shoulder from his grip, roughly pushing him away. Looking up the street, she saw no one. She could feel sweat rolling down her back.

Another man emerged from the saloon and headed toward her. Clutching her satchel, Flora began running down the street, yelling "Help!" at the top of her lungs. Her would-be attackers slunk off in the shadows, anxious to be away from this female's blood-curdling screams.

She paused at a junction to catch her breath and noticed two uniformed officers in front of an ugly red brick building. She headed toward them and, as she drew nearer, she could see them pointing at her. She slowed and reached up to her unruly hair; she must look a sight. Embarrassed, she stopped and tucked in her shirtwaist which was flapping loose.

"Yep, this must be the one." The sandy-haired officer dismissed the other with a wave of his hand. "Go tell Jake to send a wire to Constable Furlow in the Heights. Tell 'em they can stop looking. Tell 'em she looks okay to me. Well, not exactly okay, but alive and kicking."

"Officer, I need to get. . ." Flora, breathlessly tried to speak.

"Yes, ma'am, we know. You're Flora Logan, and your father wants you back in Houston."

As she realized what must have happened, she felt relief and fear in equal proportions. "My father is looking for me?"

"That's right, ma'am, him and the rest of Harris County. Now where's the friend you ran off with? He left you already?"

"No one was with me. I didn't run away. I don't know what you mean."

"Miss, the train porter saw you leave with a man. You might as well give us his name."

"No, I just needed a ride to the Thicket so I could . . ."

For the next hour Flora repeated her story again and again to the officers who shook their heads in disgust.

"Well, we found you. Why he wants you back, I don't know. But, we get the reward."

The taller of the officers answered a crisp knock at the door. Returning, he said, "We're gonna take you back, but not tonight."

"Where's she gonna stay?" the officer asked.

"That's what I'm telling you. Jake just got an answer to our wire. Miss Logan, your father says, and I quote,'Let her spend the night in jail.'" He frowned as if she were a problem case. "You wayward girls have got to learn."

Flora looked at him speechless for a moment or two, lifted her shoulders, and announced haughtily, "Well, sir, that statement confirms my opinion of the male population." She stood and asked, "Would you please show me to my accommodations so that I may freshen up?"

As she sat on the narrow cot in her cell, Flora thought about what had happened to her, and had to admit it stemmed from her own actions. She had planned this trip expecting difficulties but willing to meet the problems in order to achieve her goal. She didn't want to stay home and cook and sew, or go out only to attend church or a tea party. She tried to feel remorse, but instead she felt satisfaction with what she had done. Her father would expect her to be penitent, not angry that just being female had caused her predicament. She spent a sleepless night dreading going home.

The next afternoon the train clattered down the track too quickly, carrying Flora back to Houston. She dreaded her father's rage, but she was determined not to let him break her. "I am who I am, and he must let me go and let me be."

It was eight p.m. when she got off the train. Fred Logan was standing on the platform. His grim face and thundering eyes were no surprise. He silently took her arm and handed an envelope of money to the officer who'd escorted her. They left the station and headed for home.

Her mother waited on the porch wringing her hands. Next to her was cousin Caleb looking worried and scared. Flora reached out to her mother, seeking comfort, but Martha Logan twisted away and would not meet her eyes.

Her father began as soon as they entered the house. Again and again he berated Flora for her actions. He was incensed by her refusal to implicate the man she'd gone to meet and humiliated at having to deal with the police. Flora steadfastly refused to identify Fain, protecting herself, not him. If she named him, the gossips would link the two of them forever. She could bear the shame alone, but she couldn't bear the thought of anyone thinking she'd run away with Ward Fain.

Having worked himself up, her father listed her past misdeeds, ticking them off one by one. Flora bowed her head, uncharacteristically silent during his tirade. She spoke only once and that was to question him, "Why didn't you ask Dessie why I went to the Big Thicket?"

"I did, and she said you went alone to do some botanizing." He stopped and looked angrily at his wife, "You see what you caused with all this flower stuff?" He quickly returned to his subject, "The porter swears you got off the train with a man. I'd believe him, a total stranger, before I'd believe your little friend that's been covering for you since you two were in grade school." From time-to-time she glanced at her mother for support, but each time she looked away. Finally, he seemed through, and Flora took a step toward the back hall. He grabbed her sleeve.

"No, you don't get off with just a lecture. You have delighted in setting tongues to wag for the last time. If my wagon accident hadn't caused me to turn around and come home, there's no telling when you'd have gotten back." He was silent for a moment. The sound of his ragged breathing filled the room. "I'll not have you shaming this house again."

"What are you talking about? All I did was miss my train back to Houston!"

"No telling what sort of seed you picked up in those woods." Her father sneered contemptuously. "No bastard babes will come out of this house. Pack your suitcase and be ready to leave town at four p.m. tomorrow."

Flora looked at the rough, calloused hand that pinioned her arm, "I've been in Hell since I entered this house tonight. Where do I go next?"

He released her arm and struck her face with the flat of his hand. She fell back against a table. Her mother's handpainted china lamp tilted crazily. She righted the piece, and then stood tall, meeting his glare with one of her own.

He faltered, then puffed out his chest and announced, "I've sent word to Ruth to be expecting you."

"New York City?" she asked, staring at her father. She didn't know how to react. Surely, he would know that sending her there was like Brer Rabbit being thrown in the briar patch. How could he have arrived at the one punishment she would welcome? She lowered her lashes, fearing that he could read her thoughts by studying her eyes. She squeezed her hands together and let her body slump dejectedly. Suddenly she knew. She studied Martha Logan's face, looking at her sidewise. "Mother, are you in favor of this too?"

Her mother glanced nervously at her father, a thin smile momentarily lit her face. She wet her lips before replying, "He's your father, Flora. He knows best." Mrs. Logan bent her head and clasped her hands together under her chin. "We've done all we can to help you grow up to be a good girl who will make some man a good wife. Your father is disappointed."

She had no defense except for the fact that she didn't intend to make any man a good or a bad wife. Her father would not care for that line of reasoning, and she had no wish to cause additional trouble for her mother. She turned and left the living room, in tears for the first time since her ordeal had begun.

"Your father is disappointed," she mimicked her mother's words, and yet, she knew from experience that her mother's objective was "first and foremost to please my husband." How often she'd heard her say, "Your father looks very troubled this evening, we must not disturb him."

Flora was well aware of the contrast between the exalted status of men and the position of females. She could remember one evening last month before her graduation. She and her mother were working on the white lawn dress for her commencement. Flora, all thumbs when it came to simple sewing, much less the intricate tucks and lace insertions at hand, became impatient with the task. She watched her mother, bent over the Singer stitching up the mutton leg sleeve, and sighed in exasperation. "I want to study botany. I want to teach at Heights High." She paused to see if she had her mother's attention.

"That's nice dear." Her mother concentrated on the upper sleeve gathers. The clatter of the treadle continued.

Flora continued cautiously, "Mother, I don't want to get married and have babies and be at a husband's beck and call."

"Of course, you're scared to be in bed with a man, and all women fear birthing babies." Her mother laughed mirthlessly and the treadle continued clacking. Then the machine stopped. She turned and looked over her shoulder sharply. "Is that what you're learning from those Eastern magazines you keep ordering?"

"No, Mama, well, yes, I've read about new ideas for women. Girls who go to college receive training for a job and gain self-confidence." Flora stood and let the cloth she was working on fall to the floor. "They learn not to be duped into marriage, or if they choose to wed, they remain their own person and don't become their husband's slave."

Her mother pressed her lips together thinly. "My dear, I doubt your life will be much different from mine. Those books don't talk about what this world is really like. They're just books." Flora remembered the indulgent smile her mother had given her as she said, "A woman has to accept marriage, submit to a husband's demands in the bedroom, and have however many children God intends. We must sacrifice any talent we might possess." Flora's voiceless protest died in her throat as her mother continued with her old-fashioned drivel. "If you have a good voice, sing in the choir. If you're a gifted artist, paint china plates. It's simple enough. Lord help us if you have other ideas."

"Mother, you can't even claim property rights to this house. A married woman doesn't own so much as the clothes on her back. Father could give away your whole wardrobe, and you couldn't even file against him in court."

"Who's been telling you nonsense like that? Why in this world do you think Fred Logan would want to take away my clothes?"

"That's not the point. I know he wouldn't want to sell your clothes, but the fact he has a right to do so is preposterous. It's no mystery why ladies look upon Lydia Pinkham as a savior. Do you know how many women slurp down that alcoholic tonic?"

"Why Flora Logan, you know good and well that I took the pledge long ago. I've been a member of the W.C.T.U. for fifteen years."

Her mother had begun to lose patience, and Flora carefully framed her words, determined to make her point. "I know you don't drink whiskey, but those tonics for ladies are loaded with alcohol. I saw the president of the Sunshine Society's Sewing Circle at Red Cross Pharmacy buying Paine's Celery Compound. She has no idea that it contains alcohol; she just knows that it makes her feel better about her son that ran away on that freight train."

"Well, she does carry a burden. When her first husband died, God rest his soul, she had to marry again so someone would support her, and it hasn't been a happy situation."

"That's what I'm trying to tell you. I'm not going to marry. That's why I need an education."

"You mean you don't want to get married at all? Why, being a homemaker and having children, that's a woman's life. You sound like some freak!"

"Mother, why does the word 'woman' have to mean 'wife'?"

Martha Logan hadn't answered, and Flora had realized that though her mother could admit to feelings of dissatisfaction, she couldn't admit her daughter's right to seek a different path. Or could she? She may have engineered the exile to New York.

She pulled the coverlet from under the pansy-embroidered pillow shams so lovingly fashioned by her mother, throwing them carelessly at the foot of the bed. Maybe in New York, she thought dreamily, things would be different. Maybe New York would provide her with a place where her life would be controlled not by her sex, but by the extent of her ability. Was there a world like that? Not in Houston Heights. As she reached her room, she sank down on the bed and giving in to her body's weariness, she slept

CHAPTER THREE

August 20, 1912

Dear Flora,

On November 11th I will marry Carter Standley. I am so lucky. He is wonderful to me and Aunt Ferdie. He is a home builder in Houston Heights.

Flora, please come and be my maid of honor in the wedding. It would mean a lot for you to be here. I've missed you these past four years, and as I have said before, I still feel to blame for what happened. If only you had not gone alone.

You would be proud of the Heights. I know we sound like hicks compared to New York City, but our friendly city just keeps on growing.

Your dad's marble company has been awarded a big contract to do some of the stone work for the Rice Hotel's interior. A man named Jesse Jones is building it and is spending $2,000,000! Can you imagine that much money here in Houston?

Please think about coming and let me know as soon as possible.

Your devoted friend,
Dessie Trichelle

Flora shook her head and smiled at her friend's light-hearted but earnest words. It would be fun to be there for Dessie's wedding, but she had not returned to Houston even for her mother's funeral.

She never dreamed when she left that day in May that she would not see her mother again. Their parting was a bittersweet memory. A stiff hug between mother and daughter on the train depot's platform, her father standing next to them, his head held high, his eyes full of anger. The conductor helping her up the steps as he called "all aboard" to the straggling passengers. Once inside Flora had rushed to the window, opened the glass, watching as the hissing steam swirled around her father's tall bulky frame and the small figure dressed in navy blue crepe de chine, her prized cameo brooch pinned to the neck of her lace collar. Martha Logan was almost hidden from view, and then she stepped out of a cloud of billowing smoke and reached out her arms, the tears running down her cheeks, as the train pulled out of the station. Those tears would remain the last memories she had of this woman whose passion for flowers had prompted her to name her only daughter Flora.

"Flora, Flora, are you home?" She could hear Aunt Ruth coming in the front door.

Aunt Ruth set a mesh bag filled with brown paper parcels on the table. "I just bought a couple of lamb chops and some fresh green beans for our supper. You haven't eaten, have you?"

"No, Aunt Ruth." Flora kissed the soft lavender-scented cheek and handed her Dessie's letter.

Ruth scanned the rounded girlish script and said, "Ah, little Dessie's getting married. And how do you feel about that, Miss Independence?"

"Aunt Ruth, I'm happy for Dessie. She'll make a wonderful wife and mother and will enjoy doing it." Flora answered, "I'm not against matrimony for everyone, just for myself." Putting her hands on her hips, she frowned at her aunt. "I don't want a master; my father taught me how a master acts. I would rather die than be an unpaid housekeeper for a man who pretends to be my helpmate."

"Flora, you don't have to convince me. My 'master' was as good as a husband could be, but I fought him, and I never obeyed his will. Economic dependence is a terrible problem for women. I was lucky to escape it."

"You were lucky your husband left you this apartment building so you could support yourself, but you've worked hard and managed your money shrewdly, and your wealth is yours." Flora looked at her aunt with admiration. "I have come to believe financial independence is as important for a woman as having the vote."

"Oh! When did you decide this, my dear?" Aunt Ruth asked.

"When I realized that my job at the New York Botanical Gardens doesn't pay me enough for clothes, much less room and board." Flora stomped her foot. "How can I be self-support-ing? Why didn't you make me study nursing or typewriting?"

"Snowflakes and soot! You haven't the temperament for nursing. You're too bold and opinionated." Flora flushed as she felt her aunt's keen eyes. "Success in nursing depends on pleas-ing the doctors, and you haven't an inkling of what a master is until you've been around one of them. They're worse than any Oriental potentate!"

"But what'll I do?"

"I'm not sure, but I'm not getting any younger and you're my only heir. I have loved having you here, and if you don't mind staying and helping me, you'll inherit what I have."

"Oh, Aunt Ruth, I don't want to live my life waiting for a dead man's shoes." Afraid she had offended her, Flora contin-ued more meekly. "I'm living on your charity, and regardless of how kindly it's administered, I'm still beholden to you. You un-derstand what I mean, don't you?"

"Yes, dear, I do. But I don't know how to help you achieve what you want. It isn't easy for a woman to be economically successful." She sighed dispiritedly. "A woman's training is de-signed to help her do what nature supposedly intended and very little else."

"Yes, I know, get a husband, keep house, and rear chil-dren, in just that order." Flora kicked the cabbage rose-pat-terned carpet.

"There's someone at the door, go see who it is. Probably Miss Lillian's lost her key again. I'll start dinner." Aunt Ruth's words trailed in the distance as she bustled off to the kitchen with her groceries.

When she opened the door, a uniformed boy handed Flora a telegram. She fished in her pocket and handed him a penny for a tip. Closing the door, she slit the yellow envelope, calling out to her aunt, "It's a wire so you know it's bad news."

"What now? Seems like we've had a run of bad luck in our family."

"Hush, that's tempting God." Flora read the words and recoiled. Her legs buckled and she slumped into a nearby chair. She could hear Aunt Ruth calling to her, but she was unable to answer. As she sat there, all she heard was his voice impatiently calling her name. How could he be gone? She'd just read Dessie's letter telling her how successful he was. Her eyes went again to the words, and she looked up at Ruth who had come to see why she hadn't answered. She handed her the wire.

```
Western Union Telegram
September 10, 1912

From: Caleb Logan
Houston Heights, Texas

To: Flora Logan
635 East Forty-Second #102
New York City, New York

Fred Logan died yesterday. Cannot
delay funeral. Please come home as soon as
possible. We have a disaster.
```

Ruth read the words aloud and her doing so seemed to make the death a reality for Flora. She took the linen handkerchief which her aunt handed her and whispered the last word in the wire, "disaster." How had her father died? Why didn't Caleb say? "A letter and a telegram in one day, both making the same request. What a strange coincidence, don't you think?" Flora whispered.

She looked up and saw how sad her aunt looked. "I'm sorry, I haven't considered your loss. He was the last of the Logan brothers, wasn't he?"

"My dear, ominous though this may seem, you must return to Texas. Go and face the past you left behind you."

"I suppose you're right. I'll go to the telegraph office after dinner and wire Caleb. After the parade in the morning I'll ask Mrs. Britton for a leave of absence."

"Oh, that's right. I'd forgotten the Suffrage parade."

"After I wire Caleb, I must go to the YWCA and help make corsages for the marchers."

"Oh, Flora. Just ring them up on the telephone and say you can't come. You can't do that now."

"No, this will be good for me. Besides they're counting on

me to be there. They need all the encouragement we can give them."

As she entered the YWCA, Flora smiled at the scene before her. A group of young women sat in a circle on the floor of the front parlor, yellow daisies spread at their feet. Yellow, the color of the cause.

"Oh, Flora, there you are. We don't know how to make corsages. How big should they be? Come show us what to do." A plump blue-eyed girl looked up and scooted over to make room for her to sit. "Do you have a yellow dress to wear for tomorrow? I don't, but I have a wide yellow ribbon that I'm wearing over my shoulder and across the front of my shirtwaist." She patted Flora's shoulder as she sat down and asked anxiously, "Is that okay?"

"Of course, Molly, it'll look swell. What about you, Marian, are you ready to march?"

"I don't have anything yellow." Marian, a thin-faced young woman spoke waspishly. "It's probably going to rain, and I always catch a cold when it rains." Her red nose and puffy eyelids lent credence to her words. She continued her whining, "I'll have to miss the whole day to march in this parade, and if I get sick to boot, I'll lose my job. I know it."

"Marian, here's an extra yellow sash for you to wear." She tried to think how to raise the spirits of the homely, sallow-faced young woman. "It's not going to rain tomorrow, and think about the importance of this event! It will affect your life forever."

"Oh, yeah, sure. If my papa knew what I was doing, he'd bring me back to the farm fast. I hope none of those photographers catch me in any newspaper pictures. My goose'll be cooked."

"Do you really think your family would like to do without the money you send them? I think you have more freedom than you realize." Flora looked around the circle at the rest of the workers. "Don't forget, it's up to you girls to "suffer" with the rest of us for the cause of democracy."

The girls at the Y were working class women with little education and not much future. It was hard to make them realize what a difference women voting could make. Flora was convinced women voters could promote legislation to improve factory conditions, child welfare, and even the end of wars. The tragic fire at the Triangle shirtwaist factory the year before had been an impetus for these women to join their cause. Flora knew they all still remembered the front page story with its grisly photographs of the numbered coffins of the dead young girls. The parade plans of these women indicated she had made some progress.

Flora bid them good night after the last yellow bow had been tied on the last corsage, and took the trolley home to her apartment. When she arrived, she looked in on Aunt Ruth who was in bed reading the paper.

"Flora, Mr. Wilson says in this week's issue of *Puck* that when the ladies win their battle, 'elections will have to be held the first *TWO WEEKS* in November so that the new voters can have time to stop and powder their noses *and* look through their handbags while they're in the voting booth.'" Aunt Ruth looked at Flora over the rims of her tiny wire framed reading glasses. "This writer seems to think even if women can vote, they won't be able to decide who to vote for. You ladies still have a lot of opposition."

Flora shook her head as if dismissing her aunt's words. "Don't you want to join us on Fifth Avenue tomorrow, Aunt Ruth?"

"No, my time for marching in parades is over, but I'll be cheering you on. I hope they have a better turnout than they did last year, and I might add better weather. How many of you will there be?"

"There's no telling. Maybe as many as ten thousand! Some bands have promised to play. I have my banner finished. Did you see it?"

"Yes, honey, you've shown it to me twice."

"*The Times* says actress Lillian Russell AND Mrs. Otis Skinner have joined the movement. The reporter commented yesterday that suddenly suffrage is fashionable." Flora struck a Gibson girl pose raising one arm up and lowering the other dramatically behind her. "Can you imagine my being fashionable?" She clasped her hands in front of her and anxiously asked, "What if going to Houston causes me to lose my position in the movement?"

"I'm sure you can join your sisters in the Heights. If they aren't organized now, they will be after you arrive!"

The weather turned out just as she had hoped, sunny and cool. As she took her place in line, the marchers laughed light-heartedly among the ranks, self-consciously looking out at the crowds thronging the sidewalks on either side of Fifth Avenue.

After a dozen false alarms, someone called, "make ready." The band behind them slyly began a rousing rendition of "The Boys of the Old Brigade," and the women started counting time. "Left, left, left!" Several began muttering as they recognized the tune, but Flora's heart was thumping so loudly she could hardly hear the drumbeat. She proudly waved her gold satin banner with its bold black letters "Equal Rights for All," and started down the street.

Thousands seemed to be marching side by side, women singing loudly, holding their heads high, beaming with pride at what they were doing. All my life, Mother told me never to be conspicuous. She wouldn't want me here today, but nothing I've ever done has seemed more natural.

"Watch out for that corner up there, Flora, there's a bunch of hecklers," a short, dumpy woman marching next to her warned.

"How can you see anything up ahead? I'm a foot taller than you, and I can't make out a face in the crowd."

"Oh, I was warned by a lady who marched last time. There's a lively crowd that gathers in front of this saloon we're coming to. She told me they're always out there, sloppy drunk and yelling."

"Lady, where are your children while you're out here danc-ing around in the streets?" a boisterous voice rang out. Flora could see the speaker was a young man, coatless, tieless, not even wearing a hat. He looked inebriated, just as her fellow marcher had warned.

" You're joking! What kids? Look at them, Charlie, not a one of them could get a man. Just a bunch of prune-faced do-gooders. Next thing they're gonna do is close the saloons, right, sister?"

"You must be reading our minds; how'd someone that looks

like you get so smart?" The woman behind Flora answered belligerently.

Another male voice called loudly, "Look at them. They're sufrygits an' I bet they're gonna smash something!"

Flora never knew who or what crashed into the ranks of marchers behind her, but she felt herself thrust forward. Careening sideways toward the sidewalk, she lost her footing and fell, her gold satin banner becoming a shroud which draped the top half of her body.

A deep voice boomed down at her, "Jesse, I've seen lots of women try to get your attention, but they usually don't go to these lengths."

Flora sputtered and grabbed at the banner, pulling it off her head. She looked up at the man who had spoken and his friend. Both were wearing dark business suits, ties and hats. She realized they were not part of the barrel house crowd that had caused the trouble.

"Excuse me, Miss, are you okay? Can you walk?"

Flora looked up at the tall man standing at her feet holding out his hand to her. The twinkle in his blue eyes and his broad smile contradicted his concerned question. When she nodded, he lifted her to her feet as if she were a china teacup. Then he seemed to appraise her from head to toe, grinning approval.

The man he called Jesse solicitously repeated his friend's question, "Miss, can you walk?"

Struggling to regain her composure, Flora carefully took a step, testing her balance. When she looked at the second man with his finely chiseled features, she realized he was handsome enough to be a moving picture star, and she blushed, understanding the import of her rescuer's jibe. She took another tentative step and realized only her pride had been injured.

"Thank you, sir, I don't know how I wound up at your feet, but that's not a position I covet." She haughtily appraised both men. The one called Jesse was better-looking than the taller, heavier-set man. She decided immediately that she preferred the second. His wavy brown hair was blowing in the breeze not pommaded with oil and his sun-tanned face contrasted with his snowy white collar. When he smiled, his eyes crinkled and his

27

whole face smiled.

Jesse nodded at his friend."Yes, she is a true Suffragette. I wonder when we'll have our first parade in Houston?"

His friend laughed and answered, "I don't know, but I hope your new hotel is finished, so we can stand on the balcony and watch them march up Texas Avenue. I haven't had this much fun since we've been here."

Flora's heart sank as she realized they must be from Houston, Texas. She blushed that someone she might almost know had witnessed her humiliation. Reaching down, she retrieved her banner from the dust, straightened her skirt, re-fastened a jacket button, and turned to rejoin the ranks.

Max Andrews and Jesse Jones eyed the tall young woman as she marched away, her yellow suit dusty and wrinkled. Chuckling, they watched her take her place, lift her chin, and glare at them with flashing brown eyes.

A triumphant group finished the parade route, but Flora could not join their celebration. She took the ferry to the Bronx and the Gardens, quickly changing into her muslin smock and checking her pockets to make sure she had a notepad and pencil. She would wait until she finished her day's work to tell Mrs. Britton the news.

Crossing the field, she noted the gray fieldstone outlining several of the new beds she had helped plan. The upper layers of earth in the west bed had not been turned sufficiently. Too much manure was visible indicating someone had shirked this back-breaking task. She jotted a quick note. Just this side of Daffodil Hill, she came to the small rockery she had been working on. The summer blooming season had pointed up some glaring shortcomings with this section, and she had been working hard to correct these false notes while the problems were still easy to spot. The tall Joe-pye-weeds she had first seen in the Texas Big Thicket needed to be a focal point, not crowded up against the delicate Japanese primroses. She pulled her hat down to shade more of her face from the sun. I'll have to use some of my elderberry lotion tonight. I'm sure today's activities will have grown me a whole new crop of freckles.

She walked over to the outer edge of the garden and went into the potting shed, seeking respite from the sun. As she pulled down the jars of seeds, she hummed to herself and checked the wall calendar listing the seeds to be sown in September, "pansy, English daisy, and the forget-me-nots." She read the labels and put the other seed jars away, and her thoughts returned to Caleb's wire.

A four year banishment. What sort of grief should she feel for a father who had driven her from her home and caused her to miss her mother's funeral?

She had been asked to return. Why? Her father would be in his grave before she could get there. His estate could be settled by attorneys. Why was Caleb asking her to come? Why did she fear returning? She prided herself on being afraid of nothing or nobody. Yet, she was filled with apprehension as if something unpleasant were waiting for her in Houston.

Picking up the quill resting on her worktable, she opened the journal, uncorked her ink, and proceeded to enter her day's work, including the list of seeds ready to be planted on Monday. She wrote a note for whoever would do the planting, hoping it was not one of the new docents. Nathaniel Britton, whose reputation for frugality was well-known, seemed determined to get work from these volunteers who didn't even know the proper use of a spade.

She closed the shed door, and headed across the grassy field for the offices. As she walked she waved at Dr. Britton making his final run on old Bess, his bay horse ambling leisurely, sensing that its rider was never in a rush when he was studying anything here at the Gardens.

Half an hour later, Flora had signed out and placed her smock, stiff and dirt-streaked from the week's work, in the laundry bin. She walked to the open doorway of Elizabeth Britton's office and stood waiting. Finally, the tiny lady looked up from the microscope she was peering into.

"Well, Flora, what is it? Did you come to tell me about the parade? I hope it went well for you. I champion your cause even though I have no time for it."

"No, Mrs. Britton, I mean, yes, it did go well. But I have come to ask a favor." Flora began, her face felt flushed and she fumbled in her pocket for a handkerchief to wipe her sweaty hands. As everyone at the Gardens knew, Elizabeth Britton could be quick with her loud, clear reprimands.

"I got a wire yesterday. My father has died." Flora stopped and tried to swallow the lump forming in her throat. "I must go home immediately."

"And why would that be necessary? If I remember correctly, you did not go when your mother died."

"Yes, but I didn't go because I couldn't get there in time for the funeral. I'll miss my father's funeral as well, but now there's only Caleb, and he's young for his years. He needs me. I don't think I will be gone longer than a month."

"Very well, Miss Logan, I can't forbid you to go, but I do hope I will have a place for you when you return." Mrs. Britton felt compelled to add a soft threat. "There are many aspiring gardeners looking for work here even though the pay we can afford is not large." Flora thought that was a mild understatement but said nothing.

Mrs. Britton paused and begrudgingly spoke, "You have always been exceptional help. In fact, Flora, you have a talent for design work." Her words constituted rare praise. "What will you do with that talent in Texas? All you'll grow down there are rocks and cactus. Why not wait and go this winter when the ground is covered with snow?"

"I wish I could; I appreciate your encouraging words. I'm not pleased to be leaving, but it is necessary." Flora stood her ground and spoke firmly.

Elizabeth rose and in the quick nervous walk Flora knew so well, she crossed to where the younger woman stood, and held out her hand. They clasped hands, and then the petite, deceivingly fragile-looking teacher embraced her tall, strong, redheaded pupil. Silently, she turned, hurried back to her table and sat down, drawing her instrument once again to her eye.

Flora left the building wondering if she would ever be back. She had not been able to tell Mrs. Britton about her inability to go home and face her father when her mother died. She had foregone the consolation of paying her last respects because she feared he would use the occasion to clash with her once more. Now, that was over. She could never ask him why he had placed no value on Martha Logan other than her usefulness as a homemaker. Nor could she ask him if he regretted his decision to send his only child from home. She deeply resented his failure to recognize that while she'd been impulsive and foolhardy, she was guilty of no sin.

As she got ready for her trip, her actions seemed to have a finality about them that portended a termination rather than a vacation. Her departure time came, and after much hugging and kissing she left Aunt Ruth standing on the platform, her short stout figure encased in the now familiar plum-colored bombazine suit, wearing the black felt fedora with its turned up brim and spritely cock's tailfeather which she had worn when Flora had stepped off the train from Houston four years before. Flora climbed aboard, hoping that none of the other passengers heard her aunt's parting words of caution. "Don't forget to remove all your hair pins before you get in the sleeping berth at night."

She settled herself on the soft plush seat and removed her blue felt hat carefully, so as not to disturb the pompadour which she had worked so hard to create that morning. Flora smiled and patted the waves, pushing a dislodged hair pin back in place. The big city was soon disappearing, and she gazed at the rolling hills covered with morning mist. Two men seated in the next row began talking, and she gulped in dismay as she recognized their drawling Texas twang.

CHAPTER FOUR

" Jesse, the boys downtown are surprised about your eighteen story hotel."

"Yes, I'm not happy about the height. I wanted Houston to have a ten-story skyline. One of the things that impressed me during my visit to Paris in '02, was the sight of buildings all the same height. I never believed that Paris' five-story limit would be economically feasible in Houston, but I hoped that ten stories would be."

"You'd think so." His friend agreed.

"Yeah, but old Sam Carter came along and built his sixteen-story 'folly' at Main and Rusk."

"That's the one people were scared of because nobody thought you could lay bricks that high off the ground?"

"It didn't turn out to be the 'folly' people feared. He filled that building up with tenants right away."

"So that's why you're building the Rice Hotel?"

"It's time for Houston to have an impressive hotel; it'll give the town some class." Jesse lowered his voice and Flora leaned forward, not wanting to miss what he said. "It'll have five hundred rooms. I figure it'll lose money for a few years, but no sense in building it so small you have to add on right away."

"Someone saw you last spring on Chenevert Street standing in a vacant lot, pacing off as if you were measuring something." Flora heard Jesse Jones chuckle. "Are you planning to build out there?"

"I had two carloads of lumber shipped to that lot and hired a carpenter to put up a room to scale." Jesse paused and smoothed the top of his perfectly barbered dark hair. "Then I had him erect the first two floors. I wanted to feel the space for the ballroom and the reception rooms. Pen and ink scratching on architect's linen doesn't give the whole picture. I've got to feel the space."

Flora eavesdropped shamelessly, fascinated by the man who was building the hotel about which Dessie had written. Just then Max Andrews turned and saw her. His face lit up, and he smiled broadly at Jesse who turned to look at her as if on cue. The two men grinned as if they'd just won a bet or something.

"Jesse, I told you I'd see her again. Miss, may I introduce myself before you march off somewhere. My name is Max Andrews, and this is my friend, Jesse Jones." She blushed as he stared at her intently. "We've been in New York City on business and are going back to Houston, Texas. Where are you headed?" he asked curiously.

She wasn't interested in their New York activities, and she wanted to tell him that her destination was not his concern. But when she looked up at him, she caught her breath and glanced away. No man had ever looked at her like that. It wasn't a look of passion or disrespect. It wasn't even particularly flirtatious. He was looking at her as if he thought her interesting.

"I too, am going to Houston, gentlemen." Her voice sounded weak. She lifted her chin trying to look dignified, and included both men as she softly waved her gloved hand to acknowledge their introduction.

Her aloof pose was spoiled by Max Andrews' next question. "Is that your basket?" He pointed to the wicker hamper at her feet covered with a damp piece of linen. "I smell something peculiar!"

"Mr. Andrews, my basket contains specimens of herbs which I am taking to my friend Friedrick Thurow, a well-known herbalist in Houston Heights. I'm sure you have read about his work in the newspapers."

" No ma'am, I must have missed those articles. What plants are you're carrying all the way to Texas?"

He stepped back to the row on which she was sitting, reached down across her lap and began peering curiously into her basket. Graciously, Flora lifted the linen cover and moved the basket to her lap so that he could see the contents. Their hands touched accidently, and she flushed in embarrassment. When she looked up, he was staring at her again.

"I have several plants which do have a strong odor. There's Tansy, and I also have Hyssop, though I doubt it will survive in Houston's heat. It has a medicinal smell, sort of like camphor. It used to be strewn around sickrooms and kitchens to improve the smell. You might be objecting to my Feverfew. It has a lot of medical uses and can also be used as an insect repellant." She

33

was surprised at how attentively he listened to her description. She watched him reach out and touch the plants gently.

"Oh, that would be handy; cure your headache and kill your mosquitoes at the same time!" He ignored her frown. "Do you live in Houston Heights?"

"Do you always change subjects so abruptly, Sir?" Flora asked.

"Only when I'm afraid time will run out before I find out what I want to know."

"I believe that we'll be on this train for several days," Flora announced.

"Ah, yes, but the conductor may put you off if your cargo gets any more smelly."

Flora pressed her lips together and gazed out the window. As she looked through the glass, she could see Max Andrews' reflection in the window. He was pointing at her behind her back. Not bothering to turn around, she asked, "Why are you pointing at me, Mr. Andrews?"

He grinned sheepishly. "I was just telling Mr. Jones how sorry I am that I made you mad." He hung his head. "I shouldn't have laughed at your specimens. Are you a botanist?"

When Flora told him that she worked at the New York Botanical Gardens, he admitted he had never been there, nor even heard of them. She was dismayed.

"Miss, I hope you will accept my apology. . ."

"Well, they're new. Perhaps, the next time you visit New York City, you'll have time to visit the Gardens. They're beautiful, especially in the late spring."

"Even Houston, Texas, is beautiful in the late spring. Did you know we call it the Magnolia City?"

"I grew up in Houston Heights, Mr. Andrews."

"You left Houston to go to New York City?" Andrews asked. "Most of the time it's the other way."

Flora tried to maintain her composure, but she could frame no polite answer to his question. He seemed to sense that his query had been inappropriate for he turned to his friend and said, "Jesse, have you been to these gardens Miss uh . . ."

"My name is Logan, and I came to New York to stay with my aunt and study botany at Hunter College." She spoke stiffly, looked down at her basket and patted the linen covering. She pulled a book out of her satchel hoping to bring an end to the conversation.

Max craned his neck to read the title. "Oh, that's *The Harvester*, Gene Stratton Porter's new novel, isn't it? I read *The Houston Chronicle's* review. Is it as good as they said?"

"I will tell you after I finish it. I brought it to read on the train." Flora pointedly opened the pages and lowered her eyes to the print.

"How long will you be in Houston?"

Flora looked up at him in exasperation. The man just wouldn't stop. He was grinning at her again, his blue eyes twinkling, a broad smile crinkling his face.

"Not long," she said shortly.

"Max, I think the lady. . . what did you say your name is, Miss?"

"Let me introduce you to Miss Flora Logan, Jesse." Andrews answered before she had a chance to reply. "Well, Miss Logan, Houston Heights is growing, but it's still not very large. I get out to the suburbs now and then. I feel certain that our paths will cross."

He finally turned around and began to converse once more with his friend. Flora sat replaying his conversation in her mind, forced to admit that Max Andrews was nosy, overly friendly, much too persistent, but full of fun. He must be well over six feet with a barrel chest that filled out his height. She thought that despite his bulk, he looked like an oversized Teddy bear, not the usual dapper Romeo, that was for sure. Later, Flora marvelled at the effectiveness of a train ride across the country as a means of getting to know someone. At first, Flora and Max played a game of hide and seek. Flora hid and Max and Jesse sought her every chance they got. If she entered the dining car, Andrews suddenly appeared with Mr. Jones. When she changed her seating time for dinner, they seemed to know in advance and did likewise. In fact, Mr. Andrews and Mr. Jones seemed to know her moves before she knew them herself.

As they passed through Virginia, Flora had slipped to the end of the train to stand outside, admiring the Smoky Mountains. Suddenly, Mr. Andrews was there at her elbow. He pulled out a pipe and after asking her permission to smoke, lit it.

"Good afternoon, Miss Logan. Are you enjoying the view?"

"Yes, I've always loved these mountains, so lush and green, tinged as they are with this misty blue veil. Don't you find them refreshing?" Flora smiled happily at the beauty spread out before her.

"Well, yes, and no. People say the 'mist' to which you refer is caused from the hundreds of alky stills that are up in these hills. Keeping those fires burning day and night to make moonshine is what makes these mountains so smoky."

"Thank you, Mr. Andrews, for dispelling my illusions regarding the beauty of the Virginia terrain."

"Are you averse to living in the real world, Miss Logan?" Max Andrews asked his question politely but pointedly.

"That's a strange question to ask."

"I keep wondering why you were drawn to New York City?"

When Flora gave no sign of answering, Andrews continued. "I know its residents take delight in their theater district and their skyscrapers. I admit there's nothing like it in the whole country." He shook his head, and she could hear the disgust in his voice. "To me this milieu they're so impressed with is artificial. I think New Yorkers are a bunch of cold faces on the streets, and the residents developed all this cosmopolitanism to insulate themselves from the squalor and the noise of their city."

"And what will you do when your boomtown Houston becomes the same?" Flora asked.

"I guess I'll leave and go west. I have to live somewhere I can feel comfortable, and I never feel that way in New York City. Every time I go there, I can't leave fast enough."

"Is Houston the only place you've ever lived?"

"Yes, except when I went to school in Austin. Now that's a great place to live, except that it's chock full of politicians."

"What do you have against them?"

He looked at her as if studying what lay beneath her eyes. "It's about the same thing I have against the people who live in New York City. In Austin all they're interested in is the rush and fight and scramble to be first. Nothing matters but the answer to their eternal question, "What does it get me?"

Flora shivered as the train sped through the deepening

twilight and pulled her coat closer. He offered to escort her in, but she declined.

"What do you think the eternal question should be, Mr. Andrews?" She watched his knuckles turning white as he tightened his grip on the steel railing.

"That I don't know, but I've seen too many of my law school classmates, honest fellows, who stayed in the capitol, happy-go-lucky guys, grow too busy to be good to any man who didn't have the political power to be good to them." His bitterness was palpable, and she wondered what friend had been the cause.

"There's something real about Houston you don't find many places. You might want to give it another look even if it doesn't have a botanical garden." Max seemed to be trying to lighten the mood. She suspected he regretted his intimate philosophizing.

They walked back into the car and heard the porter announcing Flora's scheduled seven o'clock seating for dinner. She looked at him questioningly, and he nodded his head and laughed.

It was over the turtle soup that Mr. Andrews told her about his growing up, and the words he chose to describe his life were as important as what he said. Very simply, he told of his father's abandonment of the family and his mother's struggle to support them.

"I grew up on Kane Street in Sixth Ward, close to Houston Heights, but not nearly as fancy. When my father left home, we were living in a rented cottage that had just enough property around it for a cow and chickens and a little garden." He stopped and took a sip of water. "I was only nine years old, but Mother and I put food on our table with eggs and butter left over to sell for a little cash. We got along okay until I got into high school, and Mother decided she would get a job downtown." He paused as the train slowly came to a halt, another small town stop. They laughed as they realized that they were both holding onto their soup bowls fearful of spillage. Then Andrews continued. "My mother was determined for me to go to college and felt if she could get work downtown, it would put her in contact with businessmen who might take an interest in my education." He shook his head ruefully. "That's when she learned about the legal status of married women in Texas. Or rather their lack of status in the eyes of the law."

"I have long thought it shameful that a woman who marries has no control over her property."

"Mother tried to sell our cow and chickens and that's how she learned that she had no right to dispose of what little community property he had left behind. It was an event which shaped my destiny."

"What do you mean?" Flora asked gently.

"She became determined that I be an attorney so I could change these laws and give women in Texas the rights they deserve." Max placed his hands flat on the white linen cloth as if to emphasize his point.

"You worked your way through college?"

"That's putting it mildly. When I went up to the University of Texas for the first time, I had less than $100.00 to last me both terms." He laughed sardonically. "I waited tables to earn the $2.50 a month rent for a room with three roommates in B Hall, the dorm for the poor boys." She could feel him struggling with his pride.

"I ate a lot of oatmeal during the four years I was in Austin. I've never been able to force it down since." He looked up from his soup and grinned.

Flora laughed with him. "I admire your stamina, Mr. Andrews. You've obviously fulfilled your mother's dreams. She must be very proud of you."

"She would be if she were alive. My mother passed away five years ago." He stated the words matter-of-factly but his eyes bespoke his sorrow.

"I am sorry to have intruded on unhappy memories. Please forgive me."

"No, no need for apology, Miss Logan. She lived to see me pass the state bar and practice law. Her wishes came true. All except the passage of the Married Women's Property Act, but I'm working on that."

"How long have you worked for Jesse Jones?"

"Long enough to know I like his honesty and his style."

"What does that mean?"

"I did pretty well in school. When I graduated I had offers for jobs with gilt-edged law firms where the lights burn all night, and the ones who make partner come early, stay late and die young." He rubbed his chin ruefully. "I guess that's okay for some, and being a poor boy I shouldn't have looked down my nose at them, but I wanted no part of a firm that would tell me what to do or how to vote."

"I would be grateful just to be able to vote," Flora retorted. "And so you practice alone?"

"Yes, I'm a loner and so is Jesse Jones. Neither of us wants to be beholden to others."

"Neither of you works long hours?"

"Oh, one of us does, but it's not me. Jesse starts at seven A.M., takes a short nap after lunch and then works from two until seven. He hires employees to work the different shifts, a day shift and a night shift."

"And which shift are you?" Flora asked jokingly.

"He lets me work whenever I want. He gives me a loose rein just like he does Moneybags."

"Moneybags?" Flora asked.

"His horse! Says he's gonna make that sixteen hands bay manager of his lumber yard cause it has more sense than most men."

Flora laughed appreciatively. "What do you do with this loose rein?" she asked teasingly.

"I do a lot of fishing, Miss Logan."

The next day Flora had a conversation with Mr. Jones that provided a surprise. She was sitting staring at the hills of Georgia or Alabama, she was not sure which, when he appeared and asked if he might join her. She motioned pleasantly to the seat opposite just as the train stopped abruptly, and he slammed into the red plush chair. Seeing the polished and urbanely handsome Mr. Jones in a state of surprise, even though momentary, was amusing, but Flora wisely masked her delight.

"Are you enjoying the journey, Mr. Jones?" She asked innocently.

He harrumphed a couple of times and then suddenly asked if she were related to the late Fred Logan. She stuttered her reply and after expressing his condolences, Jones came to the point.

"Miss Logan, I am concerned because Logan's Marble Works

has a fair-sized contract to supply material for my new hotel."
He paused, and she could tell he was framing his words carefully. "Who's going to run the company now that your father is gone? Or will the company even continue without him?"

"Mr. Jones, I don't know. I suspect that's why I have been summoned home." Flora had spoken as honestly and straightforwardly as she knew how, and she was pleased that Mr. Jones seemed to nod approvingly.

"If I give you a satisfactory answer to your question, may we expect to continue under the contract as agreed?"

"Yes, you may."

"Mr. Jones, may I have your handshake on this?" She held out her hand, noting his surprise. He did not hesitate, however, and firmly shook her extended hand.

Max Andrews appeared at just that moment, and Flora couldn't help her irritation. She had wanted to ask several other questions of Mr. Jones.

"Have you seen Laurette Taylor in the new musical, "Peg O' My Heart"? Jones inquired, and Flora was glad he changed the subject.

"No, I haven't. It just opened, and tickets are impossible to obtain, or so I've been told." She looked up at Max Andrews who sat down beside her without waiting for an invitation.

"I have been a fan of Miss Taylor's for some time now." Jesse's eyes lit up with pleasure, and Flora wondered idly how well the wealthy Texas knew the New York actress.

"There's a line in that play that impressed me."

Flora leaned forward, waiting curiously, then realized Max was scowling at her for some reason.

"In this play, Miss Taylor is acting the part of a young girl in school, and finding it difficult to learn the required geography lesson, she throws her book down on the stage floor and says, 'What's the use of learning the height of a lot of mountains you never expect to climb?'"

"Why did you find this so interesting?" Flora asked.

"While I sympathize with her position and understand the practicality of what she said, it seems to me that oftentimes for the very reason she stated, we neglect to learn about the height of mountains which we somehow have to climb later on."

40

"School doesn't prepare us for life, Mr. Jones?"

"No, that's not what I meant, Miss Logan. It's rather that we fail to prepare ourselves for life." He carefully inspected his perfectly manicured fingernails. "Or more to the point, most of us choose to study those things we think we'll need, rather than looking at a world which always waits with unexpected challenges."

"That's an interesting observation." Flora nodded at his words. What would she find in Houston? She doubted Caleb had the maturity and business ability to run Logan's singlehandedly. Would the contract be lost? She wasn't prepared to run a marble business. Flora hardly noticed the departure of the two gentlemen who left her to her ruminations.

Her father had chosen an inconvenient time to die. No sooner had she thought this than she ducked her head in shame. Is it the English who say, "Death always comes too early or too late?" She couldn't remember but wished with all her heart that she had been able to make amends before it was too late. No, that was school girl foolishness on her part. Regardless of how long he had lived, no reconciliation would have occurred. Her father had written her only once since her mother's death. A brief note inside a package of her jewelry, saying that he hoped she would wear these ornaments with pride and dignity and not bring more shame than she already had. She had torn the paper into shreds and never replied. And now he was gone, and the train which had carried her away from turmoil four years ago was taking her back to a new disaster.

CHAPTER FIVE

The Missouri Pacific slid into Houston's Grand Central Depot, and Flora saw Dessie right away, standing beside a dapper young man she recognized as Carter Standley. She was pleased they had come to meet her train. Dessie, still a soft-featured honey blonde, wore her hair down, smooth at the crown with fluffy bangs, a large navy and white taffeta bow holding together her long fat sausage curls. Her hair needs to be up in a pompadour Flora thought. No women our age wear their hair down like that, but I love her navy gown. She scrutinized the straight skirt with its draped overskirt and stylish patent leather belt and wondered if the collar were made of Cluny lace.

Carter Standley, older than she and Dessie but always their good pal, was decked out in what looked to be his Sunday best. A light blue three piece suit, a soft dark bow tied under a white shirt collar as stiff as pasteboard, the slim, trim Mr. Standley was only a little taller than his diminuitive bride-to-be. A large blond wave extended from the front of his natty straw bowler pushed to the back of his head.

"Look, Carter; there she is. She's getting off now." Flora heard Dessie squealing, then saw her dancing with excitement as her fiance patted her arm calmly.

"Yes, I see. I see a different Miss Logan than I remember." Carter remarked amiably, helping her down the steps. Flora noticed him looking behind her. She knew whom he saw, and as she and Dessie embraced, she heard him say, "Hello, Max Andrews, I didn't know you two had been in New York. The news reporters must be slipping, or did you intend for this visit to be kept quiet?"

Flora hugged Dessie who began offering sympathy for the recent death of her father. When she asked for details, Dessie avoided answering. The two friends strolled up behind the three men who were now chatting.

"Sometimes Jesse just gets a yen for the big city. I merely went along for the company." Max looked over his shoulder at Flora and asked Carter, "Are you meeting someone who came in just now?"

"As a matter of fact I am." He turned around and addressed

the two women. "Dessie, my dear, I want you and Flora to meet my friends."

Dessie looked at the men standing before her, "Yes, Carter?"

"This is Max Andrews who has his law office in the Scanlan Building, and Jesse Jones, whom *The Chronicle* calls "the biggest young man in Houston.""

Flora noticed that Mr. Jones blushed slightly but appeared quite able to handle the effusive compliment. "Carter, don't believe what you read in the papers, especially a paper I own half-interest in."

Carter introduced the two men to Dessie and mentioned their impending nuptials. When he turned to introduce Flora, he was surprised she had already met both Max Andrews and Jesse Jones.

Jesse extended his congratulations to the couple, tipped his hat to both the ladies, and turned to leave. He addressed Flora before he departed, "Miss Logan, I hope to hear from you this week." Flora bit her bottom lip and nodded.

Max lingered, standing in front of her, waiting. She hoped he had not noticed her consternation over Jesse Jones' request. After a few seconds, she looked up at him thinking to herself that he looked concerned. "Yes, Mr. Andrews?" He continued to stand in front of her as if he had all day to waste. Finally, she gave in, "I am happy to have met you; perhaps, we'll see each other again while I'm in town." She uttered the words of a simpering female, and grimacing with embarrassment, she turned on her heels without a backward glance.

Max Andrews answer followed her up the platform, "I know we will, Miss Logan. I'm sure of it."

Flora, red-faced and breathless, caught up with Dessie and Carter, ignoring their curious looks. Carter clasped the two ladies' arms under his elbows and proudly walked through the station, and outside to the pavement. Flora soon saw the reason for his hurry as he propelled them to a stop before a shiny black Model T.

"Ain't it a beaut?"

"Oh, Carter, you've always been in love with automobiles." Flora couldn't help chiding him. "How about this Ford machine? People in New York get such a laugh out of the 'flivver.' Mostly, just rich people have cars there. They don't seem to pick Fords!"

Dessie rolled her eyes, preparing to listen to his spiel of Fordisms. He didn't disappoint her. "Flora, this car was made for Houston Heights. We get lots of rain here, right?" He stopped talking and gestured skyward. "And lots of rain means lots of mud, right? We're paving streets every year, but there're still a lot of country roads around here." After stowing Flora's two bags in the back seat, he assisted the ladies to the passenger side door, opened it and helped them into the front seat. "My Model T is better than any workhorse. I've carried a little lumber, some concrete blocks, a window sash or most anything."

The ladies seemed to be concentrating more on getting ready for the ride than on the enthusiastic words of their driver. Dessie pulled out her new Billie Burke riding hat, navy plush with white trimming, and put it on, adjusting the rounded crown so that it sat snugly on her head.

"I should have known you'd have one of those. They are so popular in New York. Whatever Miss Burke suggests in her newspaper column seems to become the rage." Flora checked her veiling to make sure it would hold her hat in place.

Carter finished storing her bags, reached across, advanced the spark and pulled slightly on the choke. He went to the front of the auto, reached down for the starting crank and gave it a quick turn. The smell of gasoline fumes filled the air, and the ladies wrinkled their noses. Carter smiled broadly as the engine sprang to life. "Not much cranking needed when the car's still warm." He stepped on the passenger side's running board and carefully climbed over the ladies.

"Sorry about this, but the left door doesn't open. The metal's indented as if it does." He eased into his seat. "When he designs the next model, Mr. Ford will probably take care of the problem."

They were off, turning east on Washington Avenue. Flora gasped in surprise as she saw downtown Houston spread out before her. "Carter, what're all these buildings?"

"Well now, I don't suppose I can impress a New Yorker, but I thought you would enjoy seeing how far we've come in the last four years. Jesse Jones, that man you met on the train, has put up a new building every year since 1908." Flora gasped in surprise.

"How fast are we going, Carter?" Dessie inquired.

"Fords don't have speedometers, but from the amount of rattling it's doing, I'd say seven or eight miles an hour."

The girls looked at each other and giggled like old times. "Carter, you've heard the joke about the man who named his Ford after his wife, haven't you?" Flora mischievously asked.

"Named his car after his wife? How strange." He leaned forward to hear her over the chalaka noise of the engine.

"Not at all. After he got it, he found he couldn't control it."

Dessie laughed harder than Carter, and she and Flora exchanged knowing looks. Both ladies smoothed their skirts, and Flora looked out, pointing nostalgically to the Brazos Hotel, as they turned off Washington onto Preston. "Is the Palm Court still there, Dessie?"

"Of course. It's the place to have Saturday dinner when the weather's nice. They have a new French chef who prepares the most divine Baked Alaska. Which reminds me, Flora, did you ever learn to cook?"

"Certainly not. I can't cook or sew and don't intend to learn. Aunt Ruth and I do fine in our apartment kitchen. We heat canned tomato soup, and make a nice dish with canned chipped beef. Women don't really have to learn all that any more, not with all our modern conveniences."

"Well, Dessie, I hope you don't pay Flora any mind. I like your dinners, and thank goodness, there's nothing canned about your cream gravy."

"Look, Flora, there's the Stude bakery. Remember the first time we took the streetcar downtown to go to the library and stopped there afterwards? I can still smell the little cinnamon cakes and hot chocolate."

"I wish Henry Stude had continued baking sweet rolls and not decided to get into politics."

"Oh, his speech must've been in the New York newspapers, too."

"I'm ashamed I ever spent as much as five cents on any product of his."

"Girls, what did the man do? Abandon his wife or lock up his daughters?" Carter's guffaw could be heard over the engine.

"Worse. As president of the Texas Baker's Association, he prevented the group from lending their support to the women's suffrage movement." Flora angrily spat the words out.

Dessie nodded her head, her blonde curls bouncing. "According to what I read, he told the gentlemen assembled that they should not increase a woman's burden by adding the ballot." Carter looked to Flora as if he were on the verge of laughter. She saw Dessie shoot him a warning glance and then continue sarcastically, "Oh, yes, the paper said 'thanks to Stude's efforts, the bakers of the country were prevented from making fools of themselves.'"

Carter responded with typical male logic. "Mr. Stude's not against women's rights. He's just an old bachelor who doesn't know how much you ladies deserve the vote." He shifted his cigar to the other side of his mouth and studied the road. Dessie and Flora remained silent for several blocks.

"Up ahead, it's the new Southern Pacific Building, finished two years ago, the largest office building ever erected by a railroad company." Carter waved his arms toward the building. "It even has ice water and a system that conditions the air. How's that for progress?"

"Carter, our apartment building in New York has an ice plant system. The other system isn't necessary, though I will say it does get pretty warm in the North this time of year."

"We'll make a couple more blocks so you can see the Scanlan Building and the Rice Hotel. You know ex-Mayor Scanlan died before he build it, so his seven daughters had it constructed in his memory. They hired a fancy Chicago architect cause no one in Houston's good enough for them. This building's just as plain as they are. They dress in black just like nuns, and they're all old maids, you know."

Ahead Flora could see the steel skeleton framework of Mr. Jones' massive new hotel. "That's it, isn't it, Carter?" She spoke admiringly.

"Yep, right here on the same corner where the first Capitol of Texas stood. What do you think, Flora?" asked Carter proudly.

As if in response, she rose to her feet and pointed toward the hotel. "Look, it's . . ." She sat down and shook her head slowly, staring in disbelief. "That man looked like someone I used to know."

"For heaven's sake, who? You look like you're about to faint." Dessie began fumbling in her handbag. Triumphantly, she held up a small silver vial, uncorked it, and passed the bottle to her friend.

Flora waved her hand aside and continued to stare fixedly at the new hotel, deeply shadowed despite the afternoon sun. Finally she spoke, "Carter, did you see that man standing on the pavement? He's not there now."

"It was just a watchman. See, there's a lantern inside. Caleb said there's been trouble on the job. And Tuesday's *Post* said the tinworkers have gone on strike. They're a rough group. Jones is smart to have a guard."

Flora spoke softly, watching the dark entrance. "Carter, the man I saw was dressed in a suit and tie. He was no watchman."

Dessie shook her head and clutched Carter's right arm. "Let's leave now. I don't want to be here another minute. This building is dark and spooky. I'm getting a headache." She passed some of her own smelling salts under her nostrils and fanned herself with her gloved fingers.

Carter moved the car forward, and they continued on their way down Main Street, but Flora turned and cast a long look backward.

"Okay, ladies, we're making another right turn. Don't say you weren't warned."

The Ford responded abruptly, and the ladies grabbed the vertical bar that held up the canvas top to keep from rolling out. Soon they were backtracking down Washington, and Dessie pointed to the Emma R Newsboys' home, and then Kutschbach's Florists on their right and the Glenwood Cemetery on their left. Flora could feel Dessie anxiously looking at her.

As if reading her friend's thoughts, Flora said, "This week, I will come and see Mama's and Papa's graves." Dessie squeezed her arm and offered to accompany her, but Flora declined as if she needed to bear the pain alone.

Carter broke in, "Flora, you have to probate your father's will. Caleb won't have time to do it. Why don't you call Max Andrews. He's a fine lawyer. He moves in highfalutin' circles, but he's a regular fellow, likes the ballgames, barbecues and a bottle of beer. I trust him, Flora, and I like him. You should hire him for this legal business."

Flora was surprised at his unsolicited testimonial for the ubiquitous Mr. Andrews. Carter's words brought the gentleman to mind, and she ruminated about their conversations on the train. He seemed like an interesting man who certainly had a unique attitude toward women. Was he sincere? She wondered about the book he had with him on the train, Edith Wharton's new novel *Ethan Frome*. Did he admire her work? Did he approve of women who concerned themselves with something other than domestic duties?

"We're coming onto the Boulevard. Look at the new houses that have been built since you left." Dessie began ticking each one off as they passed down the east side of the esplanade. "Watch for the blue cottage at 4th and Boulevard, one lot in from the northeast corner. Carter built that one. That's his first house on the Boulevard." Flora watched for it to appear and was pleasantly surprised to see a California craftsman bungalow, strikingly modern beside the Queen Anne and Gothic Revival style houses that surrounded it.

"There it is. He's doing another like it on Rutland."

"Dessie, hush, Flora isn't interested in home building any more than she is in homemaking."

"Carter, you're wrong. My botanical training has been used for garden design." Flora leaned forward studying a white wooden fence in the six hundred block which opened with a gated trellis. "All I've done are public gardens, but I would love to do landscape design for new houses where I could start from the beginning."

"Well, this is certainly the place. I'm telling you Houston has been bitten by the building bug, and Houston Heights puts up more homes than any subdivision in the area."

Carter turned east on Ninth and pulled over to the corner. "Is it okay if we get out here? Then I can just take your bags in through the back porch."

Flora and Dessie scrambled down and headed around front. An old woman in a rusty black dress sat on the front porch steps clutching a battered valise. When Flora realized who it was, she broke into a run, hugging her. "Annie, what are you doing here? How did you know I was coming? Dessie, why didn't you tell me?" Dessie smiled but said nothing.

Annie looked down at her satchel and shook her head. "So, you must of told Miss Ruth where I was living." She grinned at Dessie who nodded her head. "I got a wire from your aunt two days ago asking me to come here." She pulled the crumpled yellow paper from her pocket and handed it to Flora who read aloud, "Take care of my Flora. She needs you."

"I ain't never got a telegram before. It thrilled me to pieces." She looked up at Flora, her dark brown eyes sparkling. "And, well, it was a regular Godsend for me. When I left the orphanage, I moved in with my son." She stopped and took a deep breath as her chest began to quiver. "It was okay for awhile, but when I got this here telegram, I had just decided I couldn't live one more minute in that house with my daughter-in-law. Coralie never thought I did one thing right. She didn't even think I could cook!" Annie huffed with indignation.

"You have come here to stay with me? But I'll be here a month at the most. Annie, what will you do when I leave?" Flora could see that Annie was near tears and said, "Well, we'll worry about that later." She put her arm around the woman's shoulder and went up to the front door. Surprisingly, it was locked, and she stood there, wondering where Caleb was and why he hadn't come to meet her.

She was relieved to see her cousin coming up the walk. He looked troubled, but brightened when he saw her. The tall thin young man, whom Aunt Ruth said her father had formally adopted the year before, didn't look much different than when she had left home. She recalled Jesse Jones' concern as to the ability of this nineteen-year-old to run the marble yard by himself. "Caleb, you're still a bean pole. Don't you ever get a square meal?" She reached up and affectionately smoothed back the shock of brown hair which hung down on his brow.

"Sure, I board at Mrs. Wilkins, on Boulevard and Sixth. I get plenty of food, but none of it stays on me. I just run it off." He gave her a hug and brushed his lips across her cheek. "Golly, I'm glad you're finally home."

She started to take exception to his use of "home" but let

49

the remark pass as they trooped into the house. A slight mildew smell greeted them, and Flora could not hide her dismay as she saw the cream-colored canvas dust covers on the furniture. The chairs looked like seats for ghosts. Her father had only been dead two weeks, but the house looked as if it had been lonely for much longer than that.

The others began talking at once as if trying to cheer her up. Annie led the way to the kitchen, taking off her coat and hat, setting her suitcase in a corner, and rolling up her sleeves.

"Caleb, go see if you can find onions in that shed out back. I've brought a fresh loaf of bread. We'll have us a regular Sunday supper in no time at all." She turned and opened a door, studying the pantry shelves which were lined with only a few jars and cans. "Ah, here's a jar of Miz Logan's bread and butter pickles. Flora, where'd your mother keep the salt and pepper? Here they are, never mind." She put these on the kitchen table and went back to look again. "We'll have a jar of these spiced peaches for dessert." Happily, she considered the possibilities.

Before long, she placed a large platter of onion sandwiches on the kitchen table along with a dish of the pickles and a bowl of the peaches. "It's not the best meal you've ever ate, but it'll keep body and soul together till I can call up the grocer."

The lively group joked about baseball games and the activities of former school chums, and their company went a long way toward helping Flora over the initial pain of being in her home again. Annie insisted on washing the dishes by herself. "No more'n this, we'll just lay them out on a towel. Let God dry them. Dessie, you and Flora ought to go see if the bed linens are fresh enough to sleep on. But knowing your mama, I'm sure every one was folded with a sprig of lavender."

"Oh, that reminds me. My herbs, where's my basket?"

"I left it out on the back porch, Flora. Whatever's in it sure stinks!" Carter announced, wrinkling his nose.

She hurried out and rescued her plants, took them to the sink and turned on the tap water to give them a drink of water.

"None the worse. They will do fine, especially under Mr. Thurow's care. I'll get them to him tomorrow."

"Dessie, we need to go. It's nine o'clock, and tomorrow will be a busy Monday morning for all of us." Carter looked mean-

50

ingfully at Flora. "Now, don't forget my advice. It's worth something even if it cost you nothing."

"Thank you both for the tour of the city, for bringing me home, and for helping me to pass this first difficult evening. I'll think about what you've recommended, Carter."

She bid them goodnight, closed the front door, and turned to her cousin. "Caleb, what in Sam Hill is going on."

He took a deep breath and blurted out, "I think our father was murdered."

"Murdered? Holy thunderation! I don't even know how he died."

"The police report says he died from 'melancholia;' that's their way of saying he committed suicide." He grimly shook his head in denial. "He supposedly stepped in the path of the streetcar near Boulevard and First on his way home from work." Caleb picked up a black umbrella from the stand and began twisting it around and around. Then he looked up. "They came and got me at Mrs. Wilkes'. I'd just sat down to supper. It was terrible, Flora." His voice was filled with pain. "His bowler had fallen off and lay beside him. The streetcar operator was wringing his hands, his face red and angry-looking like he was scared he was going to be blamed."

"Who was the operator?" Flora asked.

"I didn't know him, but Sam Danna was the conductor; you remember Sam." She nodded and he continued his story. "He came over and patted me on the shoulder, shaking his head. You could tell he felt sorry for me since the Constable was telling everybody standing around that Fred Logan must have thrown himself in front of the car."

"Caleb, Papa wouldn't have killed himself. Wasn't he excited about the Rice? Carter says the company has a lot of work."

"That's what I'm trying to say. He'd hired a good man to manage the marble yard. There was no reason he'd have thrown himself under the wheels of the trolley. The gossips say he was drunk."

"I bet he was just tired; Papa always worked himself like a mule. He probably slipped and fell. No one would murder our father."

"You haven't been here. You don't know what fever this

Rice Hotel job has caused. It's like a 'Spindletop' for the contractors. There's millions at stake? Men get real mean when this much money's involved. I don't have a speck of proof, but the feeling in my gut tells me it was foul play." Caleb spilled the words without taking a breath. "I've wanted to say that since he died, but I didn't know who I could talk to that wouldn't think I was crazy."

"Caleb, if this is true, your life's in danger as well." Flora put her hand on his arm and shook it. "If anyone's trying to get this contract away from Logan's, won't they have to get rid of you too?" She watched to see how he reacted. Caleb remained silent. "Does Mr. Jesse Jones know about this?" When he didn't answer, she told him about her conversation with Jones which now did not seem so puzzling. "We must try to keep this contract, but we should protect ourselves. Have you talked to the police?"

"No sense doing that till I have some evidence. I'm counting on you to help." He grinned at her look of exasperation.

Flora released his arm and placed her hands on her hips. "What do you mean, I'm supposed to help? I don't even live in Texas anymore, remember? I'm no detective!"

"Well, you're here now, and unless you've changed, I know you'll make things happen." He grinned again.

"That's a left-handed compliment if I ever heard one."

He continued apologetically. "I've been too busy keeping my head above water at the office to sit down and study on it."

"Caleb, will you be able to run the yard by yourself? Can you complete the work scheduled without Papa here?"

Flora waited for his answer, but he looked uncertain and instead changed the subject. "Maybe you can find Papa's journal. He always kept one to record the progress of his work. It's not at the office. Maybe, he hid it here." He spoke frantically, and she saw his fear for the first time. "Hurry and find it, and we'll be able to figure out what happened."

"That journal isn't going to tell us who killed him." Caleb shrugged his shoulders. Flora felt sorry for him. "Of course, I'll look for it. But I hope you're wrong about his being murdered."

" Well, it don't sit well with me either." He patted her shoulder softly. "I'm going to sleep at the marble yard, unless you want me to stay with you tonight. I haven't lived here for a while. I'll be back for breakfast in the morning."

"I'll be all right. I have Annie with me, thank goodness. I don't know how Aunt Ruth always knows what to do, but she does. Take care and don't let anything happen to you. We're all that's left, aren't we?"

"Thanks for coming, Flora. I wasn't sure you would, after all that happened before you left."

Flora could tell that Caleb was close to breaking down. When she hugged him goodnight, he lay his head on her shoulder and gave a great sigh of relief.

CHAPTER SIX

Flora awakened and watched the shadows cast by the thin columns of her white iron bed. How normal it seemed to be sleeping in her old bedroom—not strange at all, yet nothing else seemed normal. Both her parents were gone, and now Caleb's questions surrounding her father's death. How could something like this have happened to her own father, and how preposterous that she be expected to investigate his death? She was curious about what had happened and felt it was awful to ignore the bizarre accident as the police had done. Their report bothered her, and she had to agree with Caleb's argument that suicide would have been anathema to Fred Logan.

Arising from bed, she began to dress. As she reached in the oak wardrobe for her frock, she appraised the workmanship of the piece which her father had crafted. The armoire had plain, narrow paneled doors with copper hinges and latches, the left one mirrored. The style was simple, like all of the furniture he had made for their home. Most of the furniture was copied from Mr. Stickley's magazine where he had ordered their house plans. He had chosen simplicity as a guide, eschewing the ornate furbelows of the Victorian style, a personal preference he had passed on to his daughter. Flora loved the curlicue white wicker furniture and stately brass and iron bedsteads, but the oversized horsehair sateen covered furniture, which was standard in most Heights' parlors, had never seemed as graceful as the straight lines of the leather-covered Morris chairs and Mission tables she had grown up with. Her youth had been spent in childish wonderment over the pastry-like concoctions which towered along the Boulevard, each vying with the other to use more spires, curlicues, and cupolas, but as she grew older she came to prefer the craftsman bungalows like the one her father had built.

She looked at herself in the mirror and wondered what her father would have thought of her appearance. With Aunt Ruth's help, Flora had come to terms with her appearance, striving to look handsome and smart since she would never qualify as pretty. The dress she wore was her newest, a beige linen with straight lines, but made in the wrap-around style which allowed room in the skirt for easy walking. She picked up a wide cordovan leather belt and cinched her narrow waist, buckling the richly tooled leather with its barbaric Egyptian designs. Much as she loved it, the belt reminded her of the horrible whalebone corsets her mother had always worn. Flora felt fortunate that these had gone out of style just as she entered womanhood. While many older women still clung to them as their shield against the ideas of the new generation, no thinking woman would now consider confining herself with this instrument of torture. Flora had no spare flesh to corset. Putting on her dark brown dress shoes with brown Lisle stockings, she looked down at the skirt's length which barely grazed her ankles. "Hope this isn't too daring for Houston."

She smiled, remembering Dessie's wonderment over her changed appearance. The reactions to her new look had been everything Aunt Ruth had hoped for. No longer the coltish young girl she had been, she had acquired polish and poise while consistently rejecting those conventions of society she considered stupid.

She removed a violet-colored velvet box from her valise and set it on the bureau. Taking out the enameled comb and brush and mirror, she twisted her mouth from side to side studying her long straight hair. She had no time to heat up curling tongs or use her Magic Wavers to make a pompadour, so she settled for pulling the sides close and sweeping them up into a knot which she secured on top of her head with a great many hairpins. The severe result was tempered slightly by the wispy sidehairs which refused to remain confined; no curling tendrils, but an attractive softening nonetheless. Taking a match from the holder on the fireplace mantel, she lit it, let it burn down slightly and then blew it out. After the stick had cooled, she applied the burnt end to her pale brows, darkening them slightly. Carefully lifting the envelope of Nadine's face powder she had brought with her, she dusted her freckles. She picked up her straw hat and a brown leather handbag and walked out into the hall.

Annie had obviously been up, working in the kitchen for some while. When Flora entered, she was fussing over the stove.

"Oh, there she is." Annie announced Flora's arrival to Caleb, who had his nose buried in the morning paper. "I'm fixin to take a pan of biscuits out, Miss Flora."

"Yes, I could smell them as I came down the hall." Flora answered appreciatively.

"Did you know 'bout this new lard called Crisco? It costs twenty-five cents a can." She looked at Flora waiting to see if she objected to the price. When she got no response, she continued. "I been using it right along now to bake with and I think it's bettern 'n Cottlene, if 'n it's okay, I'm gonna order some from the grocer's when I calls them this morning." Annie looked at her anxiously. "Did you sleep okay last night?"

"I slept better than I did the last time I was in that bed," Flora said with a sardonic grin which was lost on her housekeeper.

"Where're you off to this morning? You're sure dressed smart-like." Annie smacked her lips appreciatively.

At this, Caleb put down his paper and gave his cousin a once-over. "I don't think I realized last night how much you've changed, Flora. I'm not sure the Heights is ready for this new Flora Logan."

"Caleb, Houston Heights wasn't ready for the old version either. Let's just wait and see. I'll try not to embarrass the family like I did before," Flora laughed sarcastically.

"The population has grown so much in our little town, they may not even notice you're back."

"Hmph, Mr. Caleb, they'se gonna notice this 'un, I jes bet and see."

Flora blushed and went over to the glass-paned kitchen cupboard, reached down a mug, went to the stove and picked up the gray enamelware coffeepot.

"Miss Flora, I hadda' got that for you. Whatcha doin' waitin' on youself when I'se here?"

"Oh, Annie, don't be ridiculous. I'm accustomed to waiting on myself. Apartment life in New York City is different from living here in the suburbs." She looked around the spacious kitchen she had grown up in, its walls lined with metal topped work counters. It seemed cavernous to her now. "That's one reason why apartment houses have been built, so we don't need servants to run our home. We have all the modern conveniences, hot and cold running water, ice plants, central furnaces, even vacuum machines. It's a very handy way of living."

Annie looked downcast. "Guess you'll be putting those improvements here, too."

"No, you can't be replaced by anything electrical."

Annie grinned, reassured by Flora's words, unaware of the ironic tone of her answer.

"Caleb, you told me last night that the executor of Papa's will moved away from Houston. We could pick a substitute easier than tracking him down, don't you think? Carter suggested we hire Max Andrews to probate the will. Do you know him?"

"No, I don't, unless he's the one I met at the Rice Hotel job. Seems like a fellow by that name was with Mr. Jones."

"Yes, that's the man I'm talking about. I met Jesse Jones on the train coming from New York. He and Mr. Andrews are friends."

"Flora, Jesse Jones is Houston's youngest millionaire. What are you doing socializing with him? I can tell you right now, we can't afford any lawyer he uses. Andrews probably wouldn't even be interested in such a small case."

"Well, I don't believe what you told me last night, but under the circumstances, I think we should spend whatever money it takes to hire the best lawyer we can find. And since Andrews knows Jones, he will have more insight into the problem, if it exists." She couldn't keep the doubt from her voice and Caleb's frown indicated his irritation.

"Whatever you think, Flora." Caleb spoke sharply."I don't

have time for this. In fact, I'm already late. The will's there in that blue folder on the hall table. Just take it to somebody and get it handled." He threw down his newspaper in disgust. "We need to be able to run the marble yard, that's what puts food on this table."   He stood and bolted from the kitchen.

Annie and Flora heard the door slam and the gate bang closed. They looked at each other knowingly. "Looks like it's gonna' be up to you, Miz Flora. Who's this Mr. Andrews you met on the train? Izzat why you all dressed fit to kill this morning?"

Flora tried for wide-eyed innocence, but couldn't keep the grin from her face. "No, I didn't dress special. These clothes are what I wear most of the time in New York City. You're just remembering how I used to look. I've outgrown braids and blue and white sailor middies." She gracefully moved her arm from the top of her gown down as if to illustrate her attention to grooming. She smoothed her skirt and straightened her shoulders. "See, no more Ethel Barrymore droop." Then she reached for her plain straw hat, its brim circled with a two inch brown grosgrain ribbon, and secured the headpiece with a long brass hatpin the end of which was emblazoned with a large yellow stone.

Annie studied her actions admiringly, "Miss Flora, you has turned into a woman of class. Did you know there's a theater uptown that gives them hatpins away to all the ladies who come to the matinees?"

"What for? I never heard of a promotion like that."

"Well, I 'spects the owner just wants to get bi'ness, but someone heard him say the hatpins were for ladies to defend themself against mashers."

"Oh, Annie, you're too much. What will you come up with next?"

"You can laugh, Miss Flora, but there's a whole lots of people's living here now, not just in Houston, but also in this here little town. Not all of them's good people. There's some bad people here too."

Flora's face clouded as she thought again of Caleb's fears, and she wondered how Mr. Andrews would react to his accusations. "Maybe he'll know whether Caleb is making mountains out of molehills about this building contract."

"Why you talking 'bout buildin' contracks, Miss Flora? I thought you said you changed, and is more ladylike."

57

"Oh nothing. I'll be back by dinner. Go ahead and call the grocer and the milkman and order whatever you want. We need to cheer up Caleb, and food will do that faster than anything for a man."

"You sure know!"

Flora gave her a wave and went out to the front hall. As she left the house, she shook her head in sorrow at the disarray of the splendid garden she and her mother had designed and planted. Unsightly weeds bordered the front walk. A lone zinnia straggled up near the front gate, but the wisteria vine circled the arched entryway, looking leafy and green. She wondered if it still bloomed in the spring. The roots need trimming I am sure. She longed to reach down and at least pull a few of the dead vines, but resolutely continued on her way up the street and over to the Boulevard where the streetcar line ran.

She heard the warning gong and ran to the corner. As the trolley came to a stop, she waved at Sam Danna, the conductor, and stepped up into the car. After depositing her nickel, she took a seat near the front.

"If I didn't know better, I would say you look like a Miss Flora Logan I used to see ride this car," Sam grinned at her.

"Sam Danna, you know exactly who I am and probably when I arrived back in town. I'm glad you are still the most reliable fixture on Car 206. It's good to see you." Flora smiled at him, then frowned and asked abruptly,"What do you know about my father's death, Sam?"

"Don't know much. Mr. Logan always rode the five o'clock trolley, but he was late that night coming from the marble yard. He must've been detained, though the police didn't bother to find out why." Sam eyed the man sitting opposite Flora who seemed to be dozing. "All the officers agreed your papa threw himself in front of the streetcar. No one questioned why he would have done such a thing. They called it nerves or something."

"Had he seemed depressed to you, Sam?"

"Not at all. I was surprised the constable didn't question me since I saw Mr. Logan twice a day, Monday through Satur-day. I guess it wouldn't have mattered one way or the other. Dead is dead. Just seemed funny to me. Not like your papa at all."

"Sam, that's what Caleb says. He won't accept the melancholia verdict."

"What can he do about it? It happened only two weeks ago, but no one even mentions it anymore."

"Well, we'll see. Maybe I can help him figure it out."

Sam cocked his head and looked at her dubiously. "You're not going to investigate your papa's death, are you?"

Flora didn't answer his question, but instead asked,"You think he could have been pushed, Sam?"

"Oh, I wouldn't want to say that, Miss Logan." Sam looked around the car as if checking on the other passengers.

Flora sensed that she had asked all she could for the time being. Mr. Danna's uneasiness indicated that the trolley employees had been warned not to discuss the accident. She changed the subject, "I need to go to the Scanlan Building; don't let me miss my stop."

Sam looked relieved and moved down the aisle, collecting tokens, and exchanging pleasantries. Soon, he called out "Main Street!" He leaned over to Flora, patted her shoulder, "That's you. Have a nice visit while you're here."

She bid him good day and exited the streetcar. As she neared the building where Max Andrews had his offices, she thought about Carter Standley's remarks. The Scanlan Building, rectangular-shaped and made of light-colored brick, had the look of a monument. She wondered if that's what the sisters had told the architect. She could imagine them saying, "Make it like a giant tombstone, so Father will be pleased."

She entered and read the directory printed on the front wall. The man she sought occupied office number 310. She went up to the third floor, her heels echoing loudly down the white tiled hall. A frosted glass door painted with gilded letters announced "Max Andrews, Attorney-at-Law," and she entered a spacious waiting room. An oak library table stacked with magazines and newspapers provided a base for an unlit electric lamp. A telephone instrument mounted on a large wooden box hung on the wall beside a door marked 'private.'

As her eyes adjusted to the light, Flora realized that the room was not empty. A mousy looking blonde woman sat at a desk occupied by a typewriting machine. Wearing a starched white waist and black gabardine skirt, she sat in a straight-backed wooden chair and pondered the keys in front of her as if they were embossed with hieroglyphics instead of the English alphabet. Looking up at Flora, she smiled weakly and asked in a quiet voice, "Are you here to see Mr. Andrews?"

"Yes, I am."

"Whom shall I tell him is calling?"

At that moment the door to the inner office opened, and Max Andrews appeared with a tall, beautifully dressed, very attractive woman. Flora unconsciously appraised the lady, that's a New York suit or I'll eat my hat. The slender brunette was dressed in teal blue, a long gored skirt and a cutaway jacket. Her lacy cream-colored blouse was a feminine touch. She wore a matching bluegreen toque with an oversized satin bow which covered the entire hat and added at least five inches to her height. She's as tall as I am, but she doesn't care. Max and the lady appeared to have been laughing about something, and she noticed they looked at each other fondly.

Flora flushed beet red and wished she were someplace else. Max Andrews saw her at that moment. "Miss Logan, this is a surprise. I'm happy to see you. Are you already feeling the effects of our hot Texas sun? You're so red in the face. Surely, you haven't had a chance to go to the beach yet?"

"Not hardly, since I arrived on the same train that you did yesterday." Flora answered tartly.

"Let me introduce you to someone you need to know. This is Annette Finnigan, founder of the Houston Suffrage Movement. Annette, meet one of your fellow 'sufferers,' Flora Logan." Max laughed; both ladies ignored him.

"Did you say you had just come down from New York?"

"Yes, it is my home now. I am in Houston to settle some family business and that is why I am here to see Mr. Andrews." Flora spoke stiffly as if emphasizing that her interest in Andrews was solely for legal reasons.

"You aren't planning to stay?

"Oh no, I hope to leave within the month." She turned her back on Max Andrews and inquired of the woman, "But tell me, Miss Finnigan, what advances have you made here for the cause? The northern leaders say little support has been generated in the South. Is this true?" Annette nodded, grimly agreeing. "I have a friend who says the workers here have been generating petitions. Is that all?"

Max laughed and interrupted them. "Annette, I told you she's one of your group. When I first met her on Fifth Avenue, she was wearing a yellow satin banner emblazoned with the slogan, 'Equal Rights for All'; she was in the parade they had with ten thousand women marchers last week."

Flora wanted to sink through the floor, and she glared at Andrews thunderously, but Miss Finnigan seemed not to notice her embarrassment. "Oh, I am envious of your being able to march. I returned from New York at the beginning of the year and have had to remain here all summer doing very little."We've been circulating petitions, but you're right in saying that the South is very backward when it comes to the movement." Annette paused and continued speaking even more mournfully. "Houston, I am afraid, lags behind other cities in our state. The real leadership in Texas is coming from Dallas and Austin. Even Galveston women give the movement more support than we do."

"I was told Ferdie Trichelle and a Mrs. Ward are active organizers in Houston Heights where I grew up."

"Oh, do you know Hortense Ward?" Flora shook her head. "Well, you must meet her immediately. She is the most remarkable woman I've ever known. Don't you agree, Mr. Andrews?"

"Unquestionably so, Miss Finnigan." He turned to Flora,"She is sponsoring the Married Women's Property Act being brought before the state legislature next year." He spoke as an aside. "This doesn't impress you, Miss Logan, since New York enacted their law over fifty years ago, but as I told you on the train, it's a law I'm very committed to getting passed." Turning back, he announced, "I intend to introduce Miss Logan to her as soon as possible."

Flora could feel her face turning red again. Every time he mentioned her name, she blushed horribly. Huffily, she ignored his warm look and continued to talk with Miss Finnigan.

When they finished, Annette promised Max Andrews that she would call soon and waved them goodbye. Flora thought it forward of her to speak of contacting Mr. Andrews even if they did, perhaps, have an "understanding." Max turned to Flora as

Annette exited, and asked, "Miss Logan, what can I do for you?"

Max guided her into his office, closed the door, and helped her to the chair opposite his large mahogany desk. Then he sat back enjoying the opportunity to observe her once more. She had been in his thoughts more often than he cared to admit since they parted at the train station yesterday. She piqued his curiosity, for she was not a girl, but also not a woman. He'd joked about her blush, yet felt it indicated her inability to control her emotions. While he would bet money she was afraid of nothing, she seemed to be doubtfully greeting womanhood. He wondered from what her reluctance sprang and what made her seem so different from other women he knew.

At thirty-one, he enjoyed his bachelorhood and bragged to his friends that he could smoke his pipe in any room of his apartment. He and Jesse had made a wager about who would marry first, and he didn't intend to lose the bet.

And yet, when he had first seen the lady now seated in front of him, not possessed of a beautiful face nor flirtatious sensuality, his heart had unexpectedly lurched. As he had reached down to help her to her feet that morning, the band's music, the marchers' chants, and the drunks' jeers, all faded away. She had looked up at him with an earnestness he found very appealing, and he had known in an instant that whatever her faults might be, she had not mastered the art of duplicity. Yet as the train had transported them across the country, he had come to feel that something painful had happened in her past.

Here she was before him, a pleasingly plain-featured young woman with hair the color of a robin's rusty red breast. Her no-nonsense straw hat was firmly in place, her simple linen frock unadorned with ruffles or drapes; she looked capable and strong rather than delicate and demure. He could feel her brown eyes studying him carefully. She cleared her throat questioningly, and Max realized he had been daydreaming. This time he blushed at having let his thoughts stray.

"Mr. Andrews, are you well? You seem flushed with fever. Can I get you a drink of water?" Flora asked anxiously.

"Please, don't bother. I'm fine, just a momentary thing." Max lied uncomfortably.

"I came here upon the recommendation of Carter Stanley. I need someone to probate my father's will. He said you would be the best."

"Well, probating a will doesn't require much skill. What's the problem?"

"The executor appointed in the will no longer lives in the area; we don't even know where he is. I think the court can appoint a substitute. Can you do this for us?"

He nodded reassuringly, "If there's no executor, the court appoints an Administrator with the will annexed. Do you want to be appointed the Administrator?"

Flora looked flabbergasted. "I didn't know a woman could be the executor of a will."

"Miss Logan, the lady whom you just met was appointed Executrix according to the provisions of her father's will."

"No father would show that much favor for a daughter, even if he had no sons."

"Annette's father had only daughters, this is true, but he trusted all three. He educated Annette at Wellesley College and had great respect for her business ability. His confidence wasn't misplaced. She's done a fine job as President of the Brazos Hotel as well as helping to run his packing house. In my opinion, no one could have done a better job, man or woman. Why do you look so surprised, Miss Logan?"

She opened her eyes wide, raised her eyebrows and picked up the folder in her lap, fanning herself with it.

"What's the matter? Don't you think a father should burden a daughter with these matters?" His question missed the mark. "Are you doubting my assessment of Annette's success?" She remained silent, her eyes now downcast. "I can't understand how an avowed Suffragist like yourself could object to the idea of a woman running a business as successfully as a man."

Flora took a deep breath and spoke. "Mr. Andrews, I am shocked by what you've told me, not by Miss Finnigan's ability to successfully run a business. I already knew women were capable of that." She sat up straight in the chair and lifted her pointed chin proudly. "I guess, it's her father's faith in her and the trust he showed that surprises me most. My father did not have these feelings for the females in his family." She lowered her voice, and Max wondered if her father's lack of trust accounted for her not living in Houston. Then she continued with more spirit. "The other thing that has me so surprised, to be frank, is your willingness to applaud the job she's done, and your approval of her efforts. While I admit I've had limited experience with gentlemen, I didn't realize men felt like this about a woman's business ability."

Max masked his surprise though he could hardly keep from smiling at her low estimate of his sex. "Didn't you listen to what I said to you on the train when we were having dinner? I meant every word, Miss Logan." He spoke as earnestly as he could. "I was not indulging in polite conversation." He felt like going over and shaking her, and yet knew that if he touched her, it would not be to shake her.

"Annette Finnigan is my client and my friend; she is also an excellent business woman." He purposely kept his words calm and passionless. "I respect her, and I like her. I don't put females in one pigeonhole. You're all different, and your talents vary from one to the next." Grinning, he tried to elicit a smile from her. "I have some female clients who are so addlepated, I don't know how they find their way to my office. I daresay they can only remember the location because there's a popular dressmaker next door."

She chuckled, and Max smiled triumphantly as if he'd won a major court victory. He'd forgotten how much he liked her laugh.

"I am pleasantly surprised, Mr. Andrews, and I feel I definitely have chosen the right attorney. Yes, I would like to be appointed Execu-"

"Executrix, Miss Logan. Now let me see the will and we can decide how to proceed."

He studied the predictable document and looked up at her questioningly. "Are you planning to run the marble business? Do you want to get control away from the Caleb Logan mentioned here?"

"Oh, no. Caleb is my cousin and my foster brother. He has a lot of ability and knows the marble business inside out, but he's very young. Mr. Jones expressed concern that he could run the whole show by himself, and I have my doubts as well."

"Well, the answer seems clear enough, to me. You are older and apparently less naive about the workings of commerce. As far as I'm concerned, anyone who has lived and worked in New York City can tackle a cage full of Barnum's tigers and come away unscathed. Why don't you help him run the company?"

She looked at him incredulously. Raising her eyebrows, she lifted her chin again. He had figured out that she did that anytime she got ready to say something of importance.

"Mr. Andrews, the most pressing problem we have right now is that Caleb believes that my father was murdered by men who seek to get the Rice Hotel contract away from Logan's." Flora paused dramatically. "I don't know what to think, but if he is right. . . well, there may not be a company to run if we don't solve this mystery."

"Oh, that's a serious accusation. Perhaps, we'd better begin by discussing what Caleb's ideas are."

She described the trolley accident, her father's booming business, and his apparent good spirits. He listened carefully, nodding his head as he thought how much he liked the way she presented her facts. "He'd hired a manager when he got the $200,000 contract to supply marble for the new Rice Hotel. Caleb says men will kill for a lot less than that. Do you believe that could have happened?" Max nodded yes and watched her eyes widen in amazement.

"It seems far-fetched to me, but not any more so than suicide. Why would my father dive under the wheels of a trolley. He had everything to live for."

"The police, I take it, have not been helpful in this matter."

"Caleb tried to talk to them, but they wrote the case up as a suicide. No one in the Heights wants to think of a murder on the Boulevard."

"Let me talk with the general contractor on the job and find out if anyone's expressed complaints about Logan's supplying the marble. I'll do a little snooping, and see if I can shed some light on this matter."

Her look of relief pleased him. She beamed like some women would if he'd handed over a diamond choker. "Oh, thank you, Mr. Andrews. I can't tell you how grateful Caleb will be. And me, too, of course."

He watched regretfully as she rose to leave and almost asked her to go to dinner and a play, but shook himself in time, and simply bid her goodbye. After she was gone, he sat back down at his desk, doodling the name of his newest client on his tablet.

❧❧❧

As she rode the trolley home, Flora pondered over her incredible visit with Mr. Andrews. Deeply engrossed, she paid no attention to the ladies seated behind her until she heard one of them ask, "This is the spot where Fred Logan fell under the trolley, isn't it?"

"No, I think it happened further down. He was coming home late from some saloon or maybe the Dick Dowling Monument Building Committee meeting. The police called it melancholia, but I'm sure I would call it drunkenness." She raised her voice and announced, "I do hope that when the Heights votes to go dry, it will put an end to this sort of thing. It is truly a disgrace the way these men carry on."

Flora turned around and gave her a withering glare. The ladies made clucking sounds and looked at each other knowingly. Then one of them asked, "Aren't you Flora Logan? The daughter that Fred Logan had to send up north?"

Flora replied coldly, "Yes, that is my name. Do I know you?"

"We have not been introduced, but I used to garden with your poor mother, God rest her soul. I went to her funeral, but I don't recall your being there."

"I live in New York City and was unable to get back in time."

"Hmm. Well, my name is Mrs. Mabry and this here is Mrs. Earl Jones. We hope you've come to help your cousin Caleb and see that he doesn't follow in his father's footsteps."

"I am delighted to have met you both. Thank you for your advice. I will share your concerns with Caleb as soon as he gets home this evening." Flora spoke with her teeth clenched, but the women took no notice.

Fortunately, the two gossips got off at the next stop, their plump corseted shapes waddling down the Boulevard, ostrich-

66

plumed hats shaking with indignation. Flora let out a long sigh, relieved that she had been able to control her temper for once. Shaking with anger, she realized that it would be impossible for her to leave Houston without helping Caleb find the true reason for their father's death. She was trapped. If anything, she owed it to the memory of her family, to clear its name of these spurious accusations.

Suddenly, she saw the marble yard, impulsively pulled the cord and got off, walking up toward the office. As she neared the entrance she was surprised to see large flower beds flanking the entrance, filled with petunias, daisies, and chrysanthemums; their colorful blooms were a luxuriant new welcome to Logan's Marble Yard. She doubted that this had been her father's idea and wondered who was responsible.

Anxious to tell Caleb what Mr. Andrews had promised, she entered and stood impatiently in the outer room. A black-haired woman lazily looked up from the magazine she was reading and smiled, "Can I help you, Dearie?"

"My name is Flora Logan. Are you employed here?" Flora asked the question in a voice which expressed doubt that this woman worked anywhere.

The woman before her straightened in her chair and slammed her *Cosmopolitan* shut. She stared at Flora, and Flora stared back. Each appraised the other stonily. Then the woman before her smiled widely and wet her rouged lips. She had light grey cat eyes that sliced upward through plump dimpled cheeks, her look was one of feline satisfaction. Flora could not imagine what a brazen woman like this was doing on the premises. Her first notion was to order her out, but knew she should check with Caleb first.

"Caleb Logan, please," she requested.

"My name's Rita Campbell. I want to express my sympathy about your father's passing. He was like a father to me."

"Oh, that must have been special." The woman in front of her looked forty if she was a day, hardly daughter material for Fred Logan. She wondered who she was trying to kid? Flora watched the woman smile and wet her lips again. "Miss Campbell, how long have you worked here? I don't think I've heard Caleb mention you before."

Rita smiled again and said slyly, "Since March. Your father hired me when he got that contract for the Rice Hotel." This said, she preened and the seams of her starched white peekaboo shirtwaist experienced considerable strain. "I just moved to Houston. I used to work in Beaumont." Flora gasped unconsciously, and Rita asked, "Have you been there? It's a great place. I like it better than Houston, but it wasn't as much fun after Spindletop quieted down."

Flora ignored her question and changed the subject. "Were you working with my father the night he died?" Flora hoped that the answer might tell her why he was delayed until dark.

Before Rita could answer, Flora heard a voice that she had never expected to hear again. "Hello, Miss Logan, I am surprised you've come back home?"

"Oh, Mr. Fain, this here is the kid's cousin come lookin' for him. Do you want to talk to her?"

Flora slowly turned around and looked incredulously at the man in front of her. "It's you!" She stared at him in amazement. Ward Fain had changed little. Though better dressed, he still looked like a fool. His almost bald head was fringed with the same soft brown curls and his light brown mustache twisted around his mouth underneath his button nose. His weak chin bobbed, and his large nostrils widened as he rubbed his hands together anxiously. How had he become manager of the marble yard?

"What are you doing here?" Flora's tone of voice left no doubt as to what she thought of the arrangement.

"Oh, Miss Logan, I'm so happy to see you. You know I thought the world of your father. He was such a fine man."

Flora could not believe her eyes as she looked from the overdressed, painted secretary to the obsequious Fain. What in heaven's name was going on? Before she could stop herself, she blurted out, "But he's gone now, isn't he, Mr.Fain? How do you feel about Caleb? Do you wish he were gone too?" She left the office hurriedly, realizing she had already said too much.

CHAPTER SEVEN

Annie heard Flora before she saw her. The young woman blew into the house like a hurricane, rattling every window pane as she slammed the front door shut. She tore off her straw hat and threw it at the hall table. Annie watched from the living room where she had been removing the dust covers and cleaning the tables. Putting down her feather duster, she came into the hallway and looked at Flora in concern.

"Don't look at me like that. I'm mad as a hornet. I thought I'd learned to control my temper, but a voice from the past brought it all back to me."

When Annie failed to respond, Flora frowned in exasperation, then gave her a tremulous half-smile, reached out and pulled the housekeeper close, and as she laid her head on her plump shoulder, the tears came.

Annie patted her back, much as she would have done a baby, and let her cry. She smoothed the fire-colored hair and wondered as she had before, which one God had created first, her red hair or her temperament. Crooning softly, she tried to comfort the sobbing young woman, "No use to cry this way. It'll be okay."

She knew that Flora had experienced more than most women her age, but something had happened today that had devastated even her. "Tomorrow's gonna be a better day. Just you wait and see."

"Oh, Annie, you just don't know."

"What I do know is that you can solve any problem that comes your way. Just study on it. You'll find the answer."

Flora looked up at her with swollen eyes and tear-stained cheeks and smiled wanly. Annie smiled back and said, "See there, you be better already." She felt relieved and when Flora let go of her, she stepped aside. "You go right in and take off that linen dress. We'll never get those wrinkles out if'n you don't."

Obediently, Flora went to her room, disrobed, and sat on her bed, trying to decide what had upset her the most: Ward Fain's reappearance as manager of the marble yard, or the reawakened memories of a tragic occasion in her life. She decided it was definitely the former. She could not accept that his being there was a coincidence.

For the first time, she regretted her decision to protect his identity four years ago. Had she not done so, he could never have gotten a job with her father. He probably couldn't have worked anywhere in the Heights. What monster had she created by concealing his role in her trip to the Thicket? Had she paved the way for him to exact some sort of horrible vengeance on her? But why would he have desired to do so? He was a meek little man, mild-mannered and harmless, or was he? She had made the mistake of misjudging him before. Was her father dead today because of Ward Fain? It was preposterous to think that, yet the idea kept turning around in her head. The innocence of his agreeing to take her to the Thicket contrasted sharply with his failure to reappear as he had promised, but did that make him capable of murder? Where did Rita fit in? Was she a motivating force or had she been duped? Flora had many questions and no answers.

She knew she must discuss this with Caleb and hope that he could understand her fears. Suddenly, she realized who else would have to be told. Since she had involved Max Andrews in the mystery of her father's death, he would have to be told. It wouldn't be fair to withhold this evidence, however sordid it might seem. How could she lay her past before him?

So there it was, her disgrace which she had thought was past might have been the cause for her father's death. Was the trolley death happenstance or revenge?

She lay down and slept. When she awoke, it was late afternoon, and she realized there was one person she wanted to talk with. Quietly, she exited the house, picking up the basket of herbs from the back porch as she left.

She walked the ten blocks, cutting across an unfenced yard on Rutland, and arrived at Frederich Thurow's nursery and found Thurow at the street bending over a patch of purple meadow verbenas. He raised up when he heard her calling his name and gave her a broad smile, which was just what Flora needed at this moment.

He stood in the rustic wooden entrance to his garden as if he had been expecting her. His snow white hair reached down to his shoulders and his long silvery beard extended to his waist. His face was bright and happy, serene like a child's. He wore his old brown canvas jacket with its deep pockets which she knew were filled with small leather seed pouches, a trowel and perhaps a miniature pitchfork, as well as small sheaves of paper between which he would have saved specimens of any unusual plant.

She had spent treasured hours here as a child. Brought first by her mother, as she grew older, she was allowed to come alone. To her, he was the essence of the natural world. It was he who had told her again and again, "let the touch of nature thrill through the full heart." The words had fallen on deaf ears until she had gone to New York and begun studying the botany courses which made her realize the complexity and power of this "spirit of nature." He put his arm on her shoulder and used her upright strength to help him walk the path into his garden. "What is troubling you, Flora?"

She felt no surprise that he had seen inside her for he had always had that power. She poured out her story, voicing her concerns, questions, and fears. When she finished, he sat and studied her closely.

"You did what you did four years ago, and you cannot go back. I suspect that your father's excessive pride was more likely a cause of his death than anything you did so long ago." He examined his rough calloused palm and then looked back at her. "You say you are loathe to reveal this secret of your past. I think Caleb's only concern will be getting rid of this Mr. Fain. You owe it to him to expose this man's duplicity. Your father's company should not depend on someone who might still be grinding an ax."

Flora nodded her agreement and then asked about telling Max Andrews. She waited patiently for him to frame his words, knowing English did not come easily to this man who had not learned the language until he landed in New York City at the age of twelve. Thurow's answer surprised her.

"The Bible says it is not good for man to be alone. I lived in the wild on a farm near Hockley for many years, a simple life with the barest necessities and no luxuries." He held out his arm and gestured at the humble lifestyle he still maintained. "Happily, I spent my time in the woods, creeks, and rivers, collecting new treasures to send to the Smithsonian in Washington and your friend Mrs. Britton in New York." He rubbed his knees in satisfaction, then frowned. "But as the years went by, I became lonesome for love and inspiration, and I married a woman who lived with me, bore my children, and worked beside me until she died."

Flora's eyes widened in surprise. He had never before spoken of a wife, and she had always imagined him to be a hermit.

"Flora, Mr. Andrews has impressed you with his fairness and his wisdom."

She blushed. "I didn't mean to act like I really know him that well."

"Unless your estimate of him is faulty, he will understand what you tell him. If he doesn't, he's not the man you thought him to be."

Flora looked down at the last rudbeckias of summer growing at her feet, their blossoms still bright yellow, but she didn't see them. They could have been beds of purple petunias and pansies; all of her being was concentrating on the words of her friend, and she felt confused and uneasy.

"I am afraid I may have presented more problems than answers, my dear," he answered sensing her consternation. "Think about what I have said. I urge you to bare your soul to this man if you think he is worthy, and if he proves not to be, you will have learned much."

Flora looked down again and remembered her basket of herbs. She presented them to him, and they discussed the value of each and the possibilities of growing them in the Heights. He seemed to think most of them would survive and complimented her on her choice of plants. As she rose to leave, Thurow stared at her and reached out to clasp her arm.

"I almost forgot what I wanted to say to you. You are trying to learn about your father's death. I must tell you what I saw the night of the accident." He paused and pointed toward the Boulevard. "I placed no importance on this at the time, and I would not think it of significance now except the image keeps returning to my mind."

Flora waited patiently. "I saw a figure walking along the railroad tracks at dusk close to the marble yard. I had just finished a tramp in the woods and had gathered some new liver-

72

worts and mosses. My mind was on my plants, and I had no interest in anything else." He took Flora's hands in his. "There was a person dressed in a long dark coat, too heavy for that August afternoon, wearing a wide-brimmed felt hat which rested on his brows and almost covered his ears. This man was not tall, and he was a comical sight, like maybe it was a youth wearing his father's clothes." Thurow squeezed her hands. "I spoke a friendly greeting, but he avoided my eyes and said not a word."

"Where was he headed?" Flora asked.

"Toward the streetcar line. I turned around and watched him head directly for the trolley."

"I wonder if he saw my father fall?" She snatched her hand from his and covered her mouth. "Or pushed him?" Flora felt her blood chill as she realized the implications of Thurow's words. Her thoughts flew to the short-statured Fain who would have been careful to conceal his identity. He could have waited for my father to leave work, followed him, and pushed him under the trolley. If this was how her father died, she promised herself that she wouldn't let Fain get away with it. She took a deep breath to compose herself so that Thurow wouldn't suspect what she was thinking. Turning to him, she said,"The more I hear about my father's death, the less I know." The look he gave her indicated she had not fooled him.

"Keep looking, Flora, but be careful."

CHAPTER EIGHT

Three days later Flora was wakened by rain pounding the gray canvas awnings which extended over the front windows of her bedroom. She sat up, her arms wrapped around her bent knees and realized she had been dreaming of Ward Fain. He had been shaking his finger as if warning her to leave him alone. Her dream did not surprise her since Fain was in her thoughts constantly. Why did the business seem to be going so well if he was unethical as she thought? Why had Rita been hired? Surely, Papa hadn't been attracted to her.

She recalled her disquieting conversation with Caleb the evening after she first saw the marble yard's manager. She asked him if he were pleased with Ward Fain's work.

"Of course, I'm pleased. We're lucky to have him. He knows how to use one of these telephone instruments to get business. It's the doggondest thing I ever saw." Caleb sang the manager's praises over and over. "He's gotten us tons of work, just over the telephone. I go out and bid the jobs, but he makes the initial contact. We're a good team."

Flora realized revealing Fain's part in her trip to the Big Thicket trip was going to be more difficult than she had thought. What if she were wrong about Fain? Wasn't she the one with the ax to grind? All she had to go on was her single experience, and that was four years ago. How could she be sure the situation which occurred because of her teenage foolhardiness and Fain's failure to return for her was a bonafide reason for not trusting the man at all? Caleb obviously needed Ward Fain. How could she destroy his trust in someone on whom he depended daily?

"But Caleb, why is Rita necessary?"

Caleb frowned and spoke carefully, "She just is; you'll have to take my word for it."

That answer hadn't satisfied her. "Why did Papa hire her? She's no secretary!"

"I said, leave off, Flora. Let it alone. We can afford her salary, and besides, Ward says she dresses up the place."

She hadn't liked his answers then, and they weren't any

74

more convincing now. She'd decided she better find the journal Caleb claimed that their father kept. She would do it this morning while she made an inventory of what furniture needed to be sold.

She arose, made her bed, and put on a faded green calico Mother Hubbard, pulling on her white cotton stockings and old button-up boots. She brushed her hair and tied it back with a green and white checked ribbon.

Annie must have heard her coming down the hall, for she was already talking as Flora entered the kitchen.

"Why you up so early? You must have one of them full ajindas you'se always talkin' 'bout." Six lidless Mason jars sat upside down draining on a tea towel as she washed the tin lids and rings. She turned and giggled when she saw Flora. "You look like 'bout sixteen, Miss Flora. Cute as a bug with all those freckles showing and that perky green bow."

"Okay, Annie, what's for breakfast? You're right, I've got a lot to do today. I am going to start in the front room and go through everything in this house. Most of it will have to be sold or given away. I doubt Caleb will want any of this stuff. I need to get organized and pack up what little I'll ship to New York. I hate to sell furniture my father made, but it can't be helped."

Annie remained silent. She poured Flora coffee, sat down in the armless rocker and began peeling the hard green Seckel pears she had picked off the tree outside the kitchen door. Flora generously doctored her coffee with cream and sugar and reached for a biscuit. Annie had laid the *Suburbanite* beside her place.

"Let's see if my ad made this week's paper. Yes, here it is, 'five-room stucco bungalow on two lots, $1600. Miss Flora Logan ph. 4897.' I hope it gets some results. It will be hard for me to leave until it sells." She wasn't going to discuss with Annie the fact that she might not be able to go back to New York as soon as she had thought. How could she leave Caleb to run things since she alone suspected Ward Fain had a finger in the pie? Max Andrews' suggestion came back to her again. She couldn't picture herself running the business, but the idea was buzzing around in her brain. She had helped with simple bookkeeping at the Gardens and had grown up knowing the marble business.

75

"You sure 'bout that? You sure you wanna sell this purty house your papa built and all yore mama's purty china?"

Unable to share her confusion about what she expected her future to hold, Flora nodded automatically and began reading the paper. After a few minutes, she stood and with heavy feet turned to the job at hand.

"You need any help, you jus' call; I'm right here."

Flora walked down the hallway to the living room on her left. The ceiling was beamed with squares of varnished oak timbers, and the walls were painted an unhappy tan. A square oak table stood in the center of the room on a dark red Oriental style carpet. On the tabletop lay one of her mother's embroidered table runners, the cream linen embossed with gothic designs in russet and brown, echoing the rug's pattern.

Overhead hung the modern four-branched brass electrolier which she had helped her father select from the Sears and Roebuck Catalog. Two Mission style rockers and a copper umbrella stand completed the furniture. Not really that much. While she admired the simple designs and straightforward style of the furniture, the end result was not a room where she felt comfortable curling up to read a book. Flora sat down on the oak banquette and listed each item on her inventory. Leaning back on the hopsacking cushions, she remembered sitting in the straight-backed chair pulled up to the table, her tablet and pencil in hand as she struggled with algebra homework. Her father sat in one rocker reading *The Chronicle*, and her mother in the other one, engrossed as always in handwork, neither parent paying her attention she would think. She could hear her father's voice cut through her daydreams, "What's the matter, Flora? You've not entered a mark on your paper for ten minutes." Or her mother,"Flora, you must learn to use your time wisely. You'll not go to the party if you haven't finished your lessons." She always wished her father to ask, "Do you need any help?" But it never happened, and as she grew older she became as reserved as he was. Occasionally, because of Dessie, she was included in a group of school chums gathered at someone's house to have lemonade and cookies and sing around the piano, but she never felt part of the group. Thank goodness, I left when I did, Flora thought for the thousandth time.

The adjoining dining room was another joyless memory. Mealtime was a somber occasion. Poor Mother tried so hard, setting a nice table, fixing fried chicken, purple hull peas, fried okra, and wonderful fruit and cream pies. Everything had to be ready at the same time, for her father believed in an orderly schedule. He shovelled the food into his mouth with no comment, and Flora never saw the heart that a man's full stomach was supposed to bring about. She felt her disinterest in cooking stemmed from watching her mother's futile attempts to please a man who couldn't be pleased.

What a contrast to the simple but merry meals she and Aunt Ruth served in their New York apartment, inviting tenants, her fellow students, and the owner of the corner deli who always arrived with a cheesecake. Dinner guests at the table, on the sofa, and even on floor cushions, all delighted to share a meal. She stood and realized there was no place else to look for the journal.

"Flora, where are you?" Annie's voice carried through the house.

"I'm coming." Flora went into the kitchen. The stove was crowded with black iron pots filled with mouth-watering contents. "Smells wonderful, but I'm going to go outside now that it's stopped raining. I'll pull a few weeds since we've had this good shower. Do you have any buttermilk? Maybe I'll drink a glass before I go."

"You must be feeling poorly, Miz Flora. I never knowed you to turn down my chicken and dumplings."

"I can't eat a big meal and work in this heat."

"Okay, okay."

Annie grumbled as she went to the icebox. "The lady next door sells her buttermilk. She makes it on Wednesdays, so it's nice and fresh. See," she proudly held up a quart jar full of golden flecked creamy milk. "They have a cow penned up in the back yard. She's proud she keeps her tied up. You know the stock law didn't pass last month. The Heights don't have no laws requiring anyone to pen up anything, except childrun."

"What're you talking about?"

"The city council's passed a curfew law for anyone under the age of sixteen. The *Suburbanite's* editor said it was disgraceful that Houston Heights has a curfew for kids but not for cows."

Flora laughed and wondered for the umpteenth time how Annie kept so informed since she could not read a word. She rose to go outside, taking a bonnet from the hook behind the kitchen door and stepping out into the backyard. The morning shower had turned the swept dirt yard into a mudhole. The sun was shining for the first time today, and morning-glories along the back fence were trying to open. She sniffed and nodded her head. Houston's mugginess was an unforgettable smell.

She hopped from rock to rock to avoid the water. As she reached the hedge that bordered the side yard, she stepped onto a grassy plot of ground. Brick paths divided the area leading to curved beds edged with stones and filled with shrubs that neglect had not altered. Bridal wreath still gracefully outlined the arched gate that opened to the front yard. Though not in bloom, its lacy foliage contrasted nicely with the two nandina bushes which flanked the entry, each full of scarlet berries and red-tipped spiky leaves. Lantana sprawled along the right, leggy branches covered with small pink and yellow blooms that were one of her earliest childhood memories.

Sword-shaped leaves plumed lushly green; her mother's day lilies had multiplied again and again. They needed dividing now that they had finished blooming. She pictured the profusion of golden blossoms that made Martha Logan the envy of the neighborhood every summer.

She thought of the beauty her mother had created, the joy she'd derived from her plants, the love she'd given them, and the reverence she'd taught her daughter for the bounty of nature. This passion for gardening had been her life. It has become my life too, but it's not enough.

Saddened, she walked to the backyard toward the pit where she could see mounds of dead leaves circling the five foot opening. She surveyed the hole, noting the glass window frame propped up with a four by four. Not a bad greenhouse; the five-foot-deep-pit had boards embedded in the sides to serve as shelves for the bedding out plants, and shorter planks for makeshift steps. The sunshade provided by the glass panes sheltered the northern exposure.

She stepped carefully down into the opening, redolent with the hummocky smell of peat moss and leaf mold. A faded pink drawstring bag rested on a thick bed of sand to her left, sitting just as her mother must have laid it. The neatly printed label pinned to the bag gave the date and variety of the tulip bulbs inside and from which gardening catalogue she had ordered them. These I will take back to New York. Even if I grow them in pots on the windowsill of the front room, the tulips will be a happy reminder of Mother. She lifted the bag and gasped in amazement. Underneath, imbedded in the sand, lay a small parcel wrapped in waxed paper. She picked it up and unwrapped the bundle, her stomach churning as she sensed that it contained what she and Caleb had searched for.

A small red leather book bearing her papa's name, its pages were covered with penciled figures, sketches and notes. Dates and jobs were entered neatly beside each entry. Her heart raced as she riffled through the journal to the last entries, dreading to read what she wanted to find. *April 14, 1912. Hired Ward Fain's cousin, Rita Campbell. Never thought of a woman in the yard, but she looks right smart, sitting in the front office; I like a friendly smile when I come in. Days don't seem so long.*

Flora scanned the rest of the month and moved on to July 6, 1912. *Had a great Fourth. Ward, Caleb, Rita and me went to Sam Houston Park to see the fireworks. Rita fixed a picnic lunch. Fried chicken was tough, but she made a wonderful pineapple upside down cake, and we feasted. A band played 'Yankee Doodle Boy' and 'The Good Ole Summertime'—the songs everybody loves. We clapped and sang like teenagers. I feel younger than I have in years. July 21, 1912: R.H. job is not right. Yankees from Dallas causing trouble. Jones doesn't know. R.W. asked how much I would pay to keep this contract. I told him not a damn dime. My work stands for itself; He laughed and said what about the slush fund. Really made me mad. Don't like this man at all, and I'll not pay for privilege of providing the R.H. with finest marble money can buy. August 1, 1912: Haven't heard any more from R.W. Job seems to be going smooth. The foreman's not friendly. August 25, 1912. Don't they say, "There's no fool like an old fool." I think I've been buffaloed; I've set a trap for both of them. We'll see what happens next. Avarice is never satisfied. It hurts my heart.*

Flora turned the page and frowned at the empty paper. No more entries, and the last detailing her father's fears and suspicions. Who was R.W.? Undoubtedly, Caleb would know. She slipped the journal into her pocket, and knelt to set the bag of bulbs in the spot where they'd been. Staring into space, she mulled over the entries she'd read. Not enough to prove murder, but information that Jesse Jones ought to have. I'll give the journal to Mr. Andrews.

She stood and climbed the wooden makeshift steps. As she neared the top, a voice called out. Flora gasped and grabbed her pocket as she recognized the figure looking down at her. Hastily, she scrambled out of the pit and onto the grassy yard.

"Yes, Mr. Fain, what do you want?"

"Well, now, I don't know. You scared the stuffing out of me Miss Logan. What a fright you gave me coming up out of that black hole. I had no idea anyone was down there." He carried a rolled up newspaper and swatted a fly which was circling. "I'm just passing by. Thought I would stop in and pay my respects. Caleb's out on a job; he'll be gone till dark. What have you been doing to keep busy, Miss Flora?"

"Mr. Fain, I'm not interested in passing the time of day with you. Please don't pretend you feel anything but ill will toward me. I don't know how you got into the good graces of the men in my family, but you don't fool me. Not for a second. You're a sneaky little coward. What else are you?"

Fain hiccuped and stuttered his denial. "Why ever would you say something like that, Miss Flora?" She dismissed his words with a wave of her hand. His mild manner dropped away as he said sharply, "You're sure smart, Miss Flora. Those Yankee schools must've done you good. Just remember men don't like to be around little ladies that think they know everything."

Flora's face reddened, "Mr. Fain, my training and my social life are no concern of yours. Kindly refrain from discussing them." She turned to go into the house.

He fell back as if alarmed by her abruptness and said coaxingly, "I'm so sorry you feel this way. After all that I've done to help you and Caleb . . ."

"I imagine that you've helped yourself more than anyone else." Flora yelled these words over her shoulder as she stomped up to the back porch. She slammed the screened door behind her and stormed into the kitchen.

Poor Annie, ladling hot syrupy pears into a graniteware funnel placed in one of the Mason jars lining the counters, slopped the sweet sticky liquid all over the wet dishcloth wrapped around the jar to keep the glass from breaking. "Lordy, Miss Flora, you sure did cause me to start!"

"Annie, that's nothing compared to the fright I just had. She patted the journal, reassuring herself that he hadn't been able to whisk it away by some sleight of hand. "Do you know if the telephone's been connected yet?"

"Yessum, there's a man here doing that just now. You might have seed him in the yard."

"No, I only saw a snake."

"A snake? Miss Flora, where's your gloves? You know your mama would never have gone in the yard without hers. What you mean, a snake?"

Flora ignored her questions as she went to the front hall where the telephone man assured her the hookup was complete. She picked up the receiver and when the operator answered "Central," she asked for Max Andrews, Attorney-at-law, The Scanlan Building.

His secretary said her boss was in court and offered to take a message. Flora gave her name and number and asked for him to call as soon as he could.

Flora never heard back from Max Andrews. She was surprised and disappointed. Watching out her bedroom window, she saw Caleb running across the back yard and going in the tool shed. She wanted to show him the diary and see if he agreed they should take it to Mr. Andrews for safekeeping. Before she could get out the door, the telephone rang, but it was Dessie, not Max.

"Flora, you haven't forgotten the meeting tonight? I'll pick you up at seven."

"What, oh, the Woman's meeting at the new club house. Yes, I had forgotten, but I still want to go. What do you mean, 'you'll pick me up.'? Don't tell me Carter's going to trust you to drive his Ford? Boy, this really is love."

"Yes, isn't it exciting? He's been teaching me for a month

now; if only I can keep those three pedals straight."

"Oh great! Dessie, why not park in front of my house, and we'll walk the eight blocks to the meeting. We'll be better off in the long run."

"Thanks for your vote of confidence. If my best friend doesn't believe I can drive an automobile, then I guess no one would."

"Okay, I'll be in front standing on the sidewalk, so you won't have to stop the engine."

"Thanks, Flora."

As soon as she hung up the telephone, Flora walked out to the shed which had always been Caleb's hideaway. The top half of the Dutch door was ajar, and she called his name but realized he had a visitor and their shouting prevented either one from hearing her. She stood near the door and listened to the stranger who was yelling at Caleb.

"You little pipsqueak, you're gonna have to go along with us. We've got you in this up to your eyeballs. Your father was paying the money every month. He went right along with us from the first, and if you try to welsh on these guys, you're in for big trouble."

She could see Caleb's face, blotched and sweaty. "I am not going to pay money to Robert Wilson, and that's final. I don't care what my father did, you won't get a nickel from me."

Flora stepped back as the burly man dressed in a brown suit and a flowered waistcoat, turned and stomped past her out of the shed. Caleb sank to the chair beside his workbench and covered his face with his hands.

Quickly, she went to his side,"Caleb, I heard the whole thing, but what he said is a lie. I'm so proud of you for standing up to him. That man was not telling the truth; here, you can see for yourself."

Her cousin raised his head, but kept his eyes squeezed shut. "Flora, I'm so scared."

"Look at me, Caleb, you mustn't believe him." She withdrew the journal from her pocket and thrust it into his hands.

His face brightened when he saw what she held, and he took the book and opened it to the entry marked by his father's bookmark. He read Fred Logan's description of what had been happening on the job site, and tears came to his eyes as he realized the truth.

"I was afraid of what Papa might have done. I knew they'd been after him, but he never told me what was happening." He gulped and wiped his sleeve across his runny nose. "Maybe because I wasn't his real son or maybe he thought I was too young. But he's the only father I ever knew."

"It's okay, Caleb. Parents never think their offspring are grownup. It had nothing to do with your abilities; he just didn't know how to share his troubles." She patted his shoulder in an attempt to comfort him. "Caleb, was he referring to Rita when he talked about the "old dog" and the "new tricks."

"I don't know. He seemed smitten with her from the first. I didn't want to tell you, but Ward Fain no sooner hired her, than she and Papa got spoony." Flora sensed his embarrassment. "I didn't know what to think. I mean, I didn't blame him; she's a real looker. I tried to be glad for him, but she seemed too young. I couldn't believe she really cared for him," Caleb blushed, "you know, mushy like."

"I would have doubted that too."

"Women come by from time to time; you know how they chase the widowers, but Rita was different. She's so pretty and she knows how to talk to a man." Caleb rolled his eyes and almost drooled. Flora realized what a pushover he was.

"Papa was referring to Robert Wilson when he says R.W. That's who he was trying to trap, him and maybe that man that came here tonight. I don't think he would have set a trap for Rita. Caleb gulped and hunched his shoulders. "I wasn't sure about the money under the table. I'd heard talk of this on the job, but I didn't know whether or not we'd been approached." He shook his head, grimly looking at Flora. "What a mess. What should we do?"

"I was coming over tonight to show you the diary and make a suggestion." Flora outlined her idea. Caleb agreed, relieved she was taking responsibility.

"I must go now and get dressed for the meeting. It's at the new club house just up the street."

"If you see Laura Brown, tell her I said 'hello.'"

"You mean the minister's daughter?"

"Yep, that's the one."

Flora grinned sardonically. Typically male, Caleb could pant for a trollop like Rita Campbell and be all soft and tender about a virginal minister's daughter in the space of three minutes.

Flora hurriedly walked back into the house. Twilight shadows hid the figure crouched in the ligustrum hedge.

CHAPTER NINE

Flora sat on the bed, the book open in her lap, her heart beating wildly, the blood pounding in her head. What force had told her to look in the front of the journal as she waited for Dessie to come? She was to ponder that question during the coming days.

Strange words from an undated entry at the front of the journal, yet as soon as she read them, she knew instinctively to whom they referred.

I've done my duty by both of them. They never wanted for anything. Can't help myself, but I can't love either one. The gal's not mine. Neither was ever mine.

The Ford's horn blared, but Flora was lost in thought as she struggled to understand what she had just read. Dessie honked again, and she jumped up guiltily, slipped the silver mesh bag over her arm and grabbed the scarf lying on her bed, winding it around her hair. Somehow she would get through this evening, come home, reread the entry and think about what these words meant.

"Annie, I'm going; leave an illumination on for me, but don't wait up," Flora called as she closed the front door. She laughed to see Dessie sitting straight as a stick in the driver's seat of the Flivver. Having stopped the automobile in the middle of Harvard Street, she made no effort to pull over to the curb.

"I'm sorry I couldn't get closer to the sidewalk. I don't try fancy tricks since I'm just learning," Dessie explained.

"Oh, I see. How will you park once we get to the club?" Flora asked wide-eyed.

"It's not a problem." Dessie answered firmly.

Flora was not assured but said nothing. She thought

Dessie's big-brimmed straw hat swathed in veiling made her look like the beekeeper at the Botanical Gardens, but she kept quiet so she wouldn't distract her. Dessie lurched down Harvard to the new club house struggling with the clutch pedal. Flora was surprised that gentlemen were standing in the yard. "What kind of woman's meeting is this, Dessie?"

"Didn't I tell you? Tonight the Heights Woman's Club is meeting with our Neaubeau club. Aunt Ferdie says it's obvious none of us speaks French. Anyway, it's a silly name since none of the girls would be caught dead with no beau. We all invited escorts, but don't worry about not having one; Mr. Andrews will be here."

"Max Andrews? You didn't invite him for me?" Flora asked sharply, "I certainly wouldn't have thought him interested in a ladies club meeting."

"Well, I must admit, he's never asked to come before. His interest is probably in the speech Hortense Ward is making to-night. Then, again, maybe it's a result of his train ride back to Houston last week."

Flora blushed and studied the dashboard as she waited for Carter to open the door. He held out his hand, and she stepped onto the shell-paved street. "Thank you, Mr. Standley. You should know that Miss Trichelle drove down Harvard Street and only scraped one Chinese tallow tree." She laughed as Carter dropped her hand and raced around to look for the damage.

Dessie crawled over to the passenger side and waited until he calmed down and helped her alight. "Mr. Standley, how could you believe that of me. I was as careful as I could be. I didn't harm your automobile."

Laughing together, the three of them walked up the new concrete walkway to the club house, a simple Craftsman style building with red brick columns and wooden balustrade bordering the front porch. The front door opened into a spacious meeting room with a sizable stage at the back. A new baby grand piano occupied the right corner of the stage. She'd heard Dessie say the cost of the piano was equal to the $1500.00 cost of the building.

Flora studied the interior of the new club house and tried not to think about the journal. How could she give it to Max

Andrews? She didn't want to explain the entry at the front when she couldn't even explain it to herself. Maybe she could remove the page she'd just read. How else could she show Max Andrews just the pages relating to the Rice Hotel job? As she moved into the room, she jumped as she heard his voice behind her.

"Miss Logan, I'm delighted you are here tonight."

"Yes, well, I'm glad to see you too, especially since you didn't return my telephone call." Flora spoke over her shoulder, not bothering to turn around and greet him properly.

"I wasn't aware you called. I haven't been to my office since this morning."

Conversation became difficult for the two were soon surrounded by other guests all chattering simultaneously. Flora leaned close to him, speaking softly. "Mr. Andrews, I found my father's journal. Will you to keep it at your office? You'll need to show it to Mr. Jones."

Max Andrews responded unhesitatingly, "Certainly. We'll talk tomorrow."

The two stared at each other as if they were alone until she realized everyone had sat down. Blushing, she took a chair on the back row, and Andrews sat beside her. Flora looked straight ahead, trying not to notice the curious glances of two women in the row ahead who turned and looked them over.

A large brunette called the meeting to order. She introduced herself as Mrs. Renn, stating how thrilled she was to be here as President for the first meeting in the new club house, and proceeding to introduce the women seated on the stage, beginning with Mrs. D. D. Cooley. Everyone clapped loudly in honor of her gift of the land on which the club building had been built. Flora let her mind drift until suddenly she heard Max Andrews' name called.

"I would like to ask Mr. Andrews to come to the stage and introduce our speaker. We have visitors tonight who may not know her, as surprising as that might seem."

Andrews left his seat and strode to the front. Flora wondered how someone his height and bulk seemed so graceful and commanding. By rights, he should look like a bull in a china shop.

"Thank you Mrs. Renn, for the opportunity to say a few

words about my estimable colleague, Mrs. Ward. She is an attorney here in Houston, practicing with her husband William Ward in the firm of Ward and Ward." He paused and extended his hand toward the front row where her husband sat. Mr. Ward stood and faced the group, beaming with pride. Max continued, "Mrs. Ward is the first woman to have passed our state bar examination, but we assume she won't be the last." A light applause was heard. "She accomplished this feat with a grade of 95." Several feminine gasps of surprise occurred. "She is here tonight to speak about the bill she has recommended to the Texas Legislature for consideration. Author of the pamphlet *Shall Women Have Adequate Laws*, it is with very great pleasure that I introduce to you Mrs. Hortense Ward."

The woman seated on the stage next to Mrs. Renn, stood and walked to the podium. "Thank you, Mrs. Renn and Mr. Andrews. I am pleased to be here this evening to speak about a subject that is important to me and to you. I am not here to criticize the laws of Texas, or suggest that they are a reflection on our men. I know that men are so happy to do anything in their power to help women and children that they will certainly want to give their assistance and support in reforming the laws that today are a terrible injustice and an insult to the intelligence of the wives and mothers of Texas." Mrs. Ward paused as a ripple of applause interrupted her words. "When a woman marries in Texas, her husband has sole management of all her separate property and all her interest in the community property. All her money, earnings, notes, securities, and even her wearing apparel are absolutely under his control. He has the management of them without her consent, and even against her will. He can draw out every cent of her money from the bank and do with it as he pleases. He may mortgage or sell every piece of furniture in the home, and she is helpless to prevent it, even if her earnings have paid for every piece."

She paused as several women exclaimed loudly. She then developed her argument giving a number of well-chosen examples to illustrate women's lack of legal recourse in regard to property. Flora knew the examples of deserted, impoverished wives hit home for Max Andrews. The speaker concluded with an appeal to the men in the room, and Flora understood why this meeting had included them. Passage of this law depended on voters' support, male voters. "Every man who has a mother, sister, wife, daughter or a woman in the world to whom he owes consideration or protection, should feel that it is his duty to do all in his power to change the laws so as to protect the weak and helpless against the legal slavery and despotism made possible under present laws. Some lawyers oppose the new measure, but most of them believe in it. A petition favoring it was circulated among the members of the Harris County Bar." Flora could see Max nodding vigorously. "Almost every man signed it as soon as its purpose was explained. One lawyer said, 'This law should have been passed when the Battle of San Jacinto was fought.'" She waited for a moment and concluded modestly. "I thank you for your attention."

The audience stood and applauded enthusiastically. Flora noticed that Max Andrews clapped louder than anyone else, and she smiled. Hortense Ward stood at the podium waiting for the applause to die, and Flora was filled with admiration for the attractive youthful-looking forty-year-old. Dressed in a lacy shirtwaist of pale pink, a darker pink skirt, with a burgundy ribbon sash circling her slender waist, she looked as if she belonged at a tea party or a garden club meeting, not stirring a crowd to endorsement of a measure to be considered by the Texas Legislature. Flora wished Aunt Ruth were here to listen to this eloquent champion for women's rights.

Mrs. Renn adjourned the meeting and the guests rose. Flora could hear two women sternly advising their husbands to support this bill. Anxious to meet Mrs. Ward, Flora threaded her way through the crowd and introduced herself. After they exchanged names, Flora said, "Mrs. Ward, I'd already heard of your work with the suffrage movement, but I did not know of your sponsorship of this bill. According to the newspaper, Texas is one of the two states left which has not yet given women their property rights."

"Yes, that's the shameful truth, Miss Logan." Gracious rather than strident, Flora surmised that Mrs. Ward's dimpled smile effectively cloaked her iron will. "But I feel confident that we will correct this during the next session. Are you a new resident of Houston Heights?"

"I'm here to settle my family's estate. I've not lived here in four years. I live in New York City and work at the Botanical Gardens in the Bronx."

"What an interesting job that must be. Gardening is one of my favorite hobbies. The only things I enjoy more are cooking and sewing."

Flora's eyes widened and her mouth gaped. "I can't imagine what you find to interest you in the domestic arts. You seem so modern and businesslike."

Mrs. Ward looked up at the young woman standing before her and said, "I enjoy being able to do it all. I derive much satisfaction from being a member of the legal profession, and I am passionately interested in the advancement of women's rights, but if those were my only interests, I am afraid I would be just as dull a person as the poor homebody who can't function outside of her kitchen domain."

Flora stared at this fluffy pink-clad women's advocate in disbelief.

"The compliments I get from planning a meal which my husband and daughters enjoy, the sense of accomplishment I experience when I have completed a garment made of beautiful cloth, and the delight I feel when I look at the flowerbed filled with red and white geraniums lining my front walk mean just as much to me as my cases." She shook her head sadly. "I see intelligent, attractive women of means choosing not to marry today, and I find it very concerning. I hope when this bill is passed giving these women more control over their property, their thinking may change. Marriage should not be regarded as bondage, but rather a partnership where both members are equal." Hortense Ward smiled at Flora. "I'm afraid I'm on my soapbox tonight. Please excuse my fervor, but it's a topic about which I feel strongly."

Flora frowned, uncertain what to make of the older woman's words when Max Andrews came up and handed them cups of punch. "Mrs. Ward, I see you have met my new friend Flora Logan. What can you do to persuade her to move back to Houston? We need her talents more than New York City does."

"Oh, Mr. Andrews, I have no talent; certainly not in comparison to Mrs. Ward," Flora demurred.

"She's a Suffragist leader and when I met her she was leading the parade up Fifth Avenue."

"My dear, you must come and speak to the club next month. We would appreciate hearing how the movement is doing in the East."

Flora murmured her thanks, grateful that others were now crowding around Mrs. Ward. She followed Max Andrews away from the group and spoke angrily. "Why do you persist in bringing up that parade every time I meet someone."

He grinned engagingly. "I love it when your eyes snap and crackle." She let out an exasperated sigh and turned to move away.

"Don't go. I expect you to realize that I find your actions admirable."

"Mr. Andrews, you'll have to forgive me, I'm not accustomed to compliments from men." Their conversation ended as Dessie came up with her friend Helen Milroy.

The rest of the evening passed quickly as Flora was introduced to those whom she'd not met, and reintroduced to old friends from their past school days at Heights High. If the club members had reservations about her, they were polite enough to conceal them. Heights society was no larger than a bandbox, and acceptance still depended on whom you knew or were sponsored by. Dessie and Carter's standing in the community was made obvious by the welcome she received. She could see, however, that Max Andrews' attention had not hurt a bit. She sighed and smiled at society's thin veneer.

Suddenly, Andrews was at her side again. "Miss Logan, may I see you home? Perhaps, we should have our discussion this evening rather than delaying it until tomorrow."

She gratefully agreed and after making their farewells, they left the club together. Both were silent as he helped her into his buggy, untied the reins and jumped up on the seat beside her. Soon they had pulled up in front of her house which was unaccountably shrouded in darkness.

"I asked Annie, my housekeeper, to leave a lamp burning. I'm surprised she forgot," Flora said, irritated by the dark house.

Opening the iron gate, they walked up the sidewalk to the porch. Flora opened the screened door and reached to twist the doorknob, but Max stepped in front of her and entered first. The front hall was black as ink, and he fumbled for a match. He struck a flame and saw the light switch to the right. Flora raced over, threw on the light and gasped.

"Oh no! What's happened?" She looked at the overturned chairs, the drawers pulled out, the wooden banquette seats thrown open, and the feathers floating through the air from torn pillows. She turned to Max, her eyes wide with shock. He patted her arm and then enveloped her in a bear hug that was the most reassuring gesture she had ever experienced in her life. Nestled in his arms, she suddenly remembered her housekeeper.

"What's happened to Annie? She would have stopped anyone who tried to come in." She tore herself from his arms and ran to the kitchen, turning on the light switch as she entered. A loud bump came from the pantry. Max gently pushed Flora behind him, and slowly opened the door. Annie, her mouth stuffed with a napkin, her hands bound behind her, fell forward into his arms.

Flora grabbed at the cloth in her mouth and pulled it out, only to be assailed by the most heartrending screeching she had ever heard. Max cut the clothesline which had been used to tie her hands, and began rubbing Annie's wrists.

"What happened? Who did this? Who's been here?"

Annie bawled louder and screeched harder. Flora got her a drink of tap water, and hiccuping loudly, the old woman settled down.

"I don' know Miz Flora. I never seen a thing. I was standing at the sink, wrenching the supper dishes, and the next thing I knows, the lights go out. I jes' thought the 'lectric was bad. I turned round to get some matches and light a lamp and realized they's men in this house. I ran to the front hall, but they's got that light off too. One of 'em grabbed me, and wrapped my hands together real tight. I found my voice and started screaming, and that's when they stuffed that rag in my mouth. It was so dark, I couldn't tell you a thing about them. I don't know what they did, but they sure made lots of noise. They must've been robbers. It sounded like they was really taking stuff apart."

Fearfully, she turned to Max. "I'll check where I put the journal, but I'm afraid I already know what's happened."

When she returned to the kitchen, her grief-stricken face was answer enough. "What'll I do now, Max?"

"What will *we* do? This is as much my concern as yours. You are my client, and evidence has been stolen from your home. We may not be able to bring action in court now without it, but I'll take a deposition from you regarding the contents of the journal. Then we'll decide what course of action to pursue." Flora sighed in relief.

"Will you feel safe here tonight? Where's Caleb?"

Annie shook her head no, but Flora spoke firmly, "Of course, we will. Caleb's probably at the boarding house. They've gotten what they came for. They won't come back."

"I'll see you in the morning at my office. Can you be there by eleven o'clock?"

She agreed and took his hand in hers as if to convince him that she would be okay. He left reluctantly, and Flora carefully locked the front door. Then she did the same for the back and turned to look at Annie. The woman was still shaking, wringing her hands and rubbing the rope burns on her wrists.

"Annie, why don't you sleep in my room tonight? I believe we'd both rest more comfortably."

"Praise the Lord, Miz Flora, I don't think I'll be able to sleep a wink, but I'd sure 'preciate staying in your room. I'se still so scared, I can't think."

Annie's snores were the only fearful sounds Flora heard for the rest of the night. As she lay there fuming with anger at her stupidity in allowing the journal to be taken, she decided that her only course of action was to visit the Rice Hotel job site. She would confront R.W. and then stop by the marble yard and pay Mr. Fain a call. Her thoughts shifted abruptly to the other startling revelation she had read in the journal.

She wondered if she were interpreting her father's words correctly. It would explain things she'd wondered about over the years: the distance that always separated her parents, and the distance between her and her father. She'd always thought if she had been a boy, she'd have been loved. His interest in fostering Caleb had fed these feelings. Now she knew it would not have mattered. Had her mother been pregnant with another man's child when they married? Had he known? Or had she

92

committed adultery? No wonder he acted so cold toward her mother. If only the journal hadn't been taken. There might have been other entries.

She was startled to realize that she was glad. She was happy that she wasn't his child. She smiled sadly and realized how his bitterness had colored her feelings about him. Who was my father? Why did he abandon my mother? She wondered if she would ever know and resolved to write a letter to Aunt Ruth. She's the only person who may be able to answer my questions. With these plans in mind, she was able to drift off and was startled awake by bright sunshine flooding the bedroom.

CHAPTER TEN

Flora slipped out of her bed and stood at her bedroom window looking at the quiet street. She wondered if she shouldn't poke around in the yard for clues that might identify last night's robbers. On the day bed Annie sprawled on her back snoring peacefully, her frizzled gray braid falling across her ample breast, her gnarled hands at rest. Glad that her companion had been able to sleep, Flora drew on her wrapper and slippers and padded cautiously to the desk in the living room where she took out pen and ink and a sheet of paper. She wrote a brief but heartfelt note to Aunt Ruth, repeating her father's words from memory and begging her to explain what they meant. As she sealed the envelope, Flora resolved to put the puzzle of her birth out of her mind until she received a reply. She had too much else that needed to be addressed.

In the kitchen all was peaceful, only an overturned empty milk can near the pantry indicated the mayhem of the previous evening. She closed the door knowing that any clatter would alert Annie to arise and be about her duties. Filling the coffee pot with water from the faucet, she struck a match and lit the stove. She examined the back door latch for signs of tampering and then carefully unlocked it, laughing at her fears which seemed ridiculous in the morning's bright light. She unlatched the screen and stepped out onto the lattice-walled porch. Two bottles of milk were waiting, still wet from the ice water vats on

93

Mr. Murphy's milk wagon. She surveyed the yard surprised at how normal everything seemed. Two blue jays were taking a bath in a washtub filled with rainwater. Annie's string mop lay propped against the steps. Shaking her head at the events of the previous night, she saw that Caleb's buggy was not under the shed, and felt relief that she would not have to explain the theft of the journal right away.

As she waited for the coffee to brew, she sat at the kitchen table and began making a list of the questions and the facts as they appeared now. She needed to have something concrete to present to Jesse Jones since she had no journal. Was her father's death a murder or a suicide? Her father's concealment of the book indicated he had been fearful of someone. Were Ward Fain and Rita Campbell trusted employees or foes? She wasn't sure. The journal established the graft occurring on the job site, and the theft of the journal implicated Ward Fain since he could have seen her pick it up that afternoon. Aside from that, she had little to go on.

The coffee sputtered, and Flora jumped to her feet and turned down the gas jet. Soon she was enjoying a cup of the brew with a dollop of cream from the bottle of fresh milk. As she sat there, she planned her visit to the Rice Hotel, deciding to go before she went to Max Andrews' office.

"Miss Flora, I slep poorly last night. I hope you had a better rest than me." Annie shuffled in rubbing her shoulders stiffly. "Is that coffee I smells?" The woman sank in the rocker and noisily slurped the cup she poured for herself. "The first thing I gotta do is clean up all this mess."

"It's not that bad,"

"I still can't figger out what those bad men wuz lookin' for. What'd they git?"

"I can't talk about it right now. I'm going to town first thing this morning to see what I can do. Don't cook a big dinner. Max Andrews asked me to go to lunch with him after we finish the deposition."

"That man rescued me. I'd still be in this here closet if'n it weren't for him." Annie beamed at her assessment of Mr. Andrews bravery.

"Well, I think I could have managed the rescue effort by myself," Flora retorted indignantly. "All he did was to open the pantry door."

"Yes, but he's such a gentleman; he just does things right. Those men was probably still here. Maybe they heard his voice and was scared off. I bet so!"

"Oh, I believe your imagination has been fired up by your experience last night."

Flora left the kitchen laughing at Annie's flight of fantasy, went back to her bedroom and dressed for town. She purposely selected a dark brown suit with a straight skirt and a fingertip length jacket which she wore over a tailored cream-colored waist. She pinned her watch in place and picked up a small brimmed brown felt hat adorned by a brace of bronze and green pheasant tail feathers that had been her mother's. Putting it on, she critically eyed the bouncing feathers, and decided they were too frivolous for today's purposes. She took it off and picked up her plain straw, securing it on her head with two long hatpins, one in front and one in back. Her long red locks were braided tightly and coiled at the base of her neck. She slicked back the sides and front with water. Picking up her leather bag, she called a goodbye to Annie, and left the house.

As she sat on the wooden trolley bench, she noticed the passengers going to their jobs in the city. It was a surprisingly even mixture of men and women, the latter of which weren't going into town for a bridge luncheon at the Brazos Hotel. These were shop girls much like the ones she knew in New York City. Some would be going to Levy Brothers, Foley Brothers, and Mistrot's, others were probably typewriters in offices.

She examined the rosy-cheeked young woman across from her, wondering if she was working to save money for her marriage or to support her parents. She thought of the popular song, "Everybody Works but Father." Flora knew many daughter-workers whose pay envelope was expected at home, unopened, every Saturday night. Good-humored irreverence might be implied by the description of the old man, "feet in front of the fire, smoking his pipe of clay," but as the women gained strength, she could see their attitude was changing to a flouting of their fathers' expectations.

All too soon, the conductor called out Main and Texas streets. She stepped off and purposely walked up to the wooden scaffolding which surrounded the sidewalk, looking to the top of the red brick structure which rose eighteen stories in the air. Impressed, but not awed, she slipped between the wooden barrier and through the wide entry. It was a grand scale Mr. Jones had measured out. She stepped into the large foyer and eyed the men going about their work. One overall-clad workman stopped and looked at her questioningly. She addressed him curtly, "I'm here to see Robert Wilson. Can you point him out to me?"

"Ma'am, you got some waitin' to do; Mr. Wilson never gits here before nine-thirty, ten of a morning. He's the Boss! He don't punch no time card like us." He laughed heartily.

Flora frowned and tapped her foot. She selected a corner spot out of the way, and she hoped, inconspicuous. The workmen came and went across the spacious lobby. Stacks of lumber and marble occupied much of the floor space. She ducked down and edged over to one of the piles of marble. Brushing off the dust with her fingertips, she examined the surface and nodded her approval. Gray carrera, just as I would have thought. Over to the right were dark slabs of black and green. Standing up, she heard two men talking and ducked her head down again.

"Okay, where's the money? What'd you collect last night from the kid?" The voice was smooth and oily.

"Boy, you gotta be kiddin'. I thought you said he'd be a pushover. He ordered me outta' the house."

Flora almost cried aloud as she recognized the voice. It was the burly man who had threatened Caleb; his words confirmed it. This could be who stole the journal. He'd been there. When he left Caleb, maybe he'd stayed and watched them. She wished she could stand up and get a look at his friend.

"I hung around the neighborhood though, and I think I found something your friend will be happy to pay for, something that's gonna be worth more to him than the marble guy's payoff."

The oily voice asked, "What might that be?"

"I'll discuss it with Wilson and no one else." He spoke adamantly.

"You always have extra tricks up your sleeve, Walters. The Boss'll be here soon, and you'll have the chance to show your stuff."

Flora could hardly contain her excitement. She wondered where the fellow called Walters would meet with the "Boss," and how she could hide so she could see what he had found. "I know it's my father's journal. I just know it." She mouthed the words and grimaced anxiously. The men left, and Flora straightened up. She noticed a more secure hiding spot and quickly moved behind some columns. From this point her view was almost as good, and she was better concealed.

Before long, a man entered the room who she knew must be Robert Wilson. Tall and heavyset, he would have commanded her attention by his physical appearance alone. He'd made no effort to pomade his long wavy black hair and coupled with a prominent Roman nose, square jaw and jutting chin, his physiognomy was striking. He spoke to a short man who stood near his elbow. Flora could not hear the words, but she recognized the man and clapped her hand over her mouth to muffle her gasp of surprise.

Ward Fain, what are you doing with Mr. Wilson? Flora noted the familiar way he touched Wilson on the sleeve, tilted his head back and answered the foreman. Then Fain called out to Walters, the man in the brown suit she believed had stolen the journal. It was obvious that they were all in it together, and she suddenly realized the extortion, the theft, and her father's death could very well be bound up into one package. The pieces seemed to be slipping into place, and Ward Fain looked like the link between the events.

She could now see Walters striding toward Wilson, grinning from ear to ear. She gave herself a pat on the back as she recognized her good fortune in coming here this morning. I can catch the thief! I know this man, Mr. Walters, must have stolen the diary.

Some of what happened next could have been avoided if Flora had kept her handkerchief to her nose as most young ladies would have done when in the presence of noxious smells, but holding a lace hanky never occurred to her. Three men carrying a load of lumber, dropped the boards near where she crouched. The dust their action circulated, filled the air. No one was bothered by the powdery dust except Flora. Before she could control it, she had let out an unmistakably feminine, if totally unladylike sneeze. While the job site was not a quiet arena, with her loud "kerchoo" an incredible silence descended upon the floor.

In what she hoped was a poised and elegant manner, Flora rose to a standing position, brushed the dust from her sleeves, reached up to straighten her hat, and addressed the group of amazed men who stood before her.

"Gentlemen, I seem to have interrupted your meeting. Pray continue." She tried for a look of innocent disdain and felt that she had succeeded when their faces continued to show only amazement and not anger.

Unfortunately, her nemesis Ward Fain walked over and began a diatribe that surprised even her. "Miz Flora, what're you doing here? You're without a doubt the most outrageous member of your sex I've ever encountered." He looked back to make certain he had the foreman's attention and then turned to Flora pointing his index finger in her face. "I know that your coming to this job site could have only one purpose: your consistent desire to cause trouble. You have been stirring up commotion the whole time I've known you." He paused, breathed deeply and drew himself up,"This time you may have gone too far. I don't think Mr. Wilson is going to take kindly to your being in this restricted job site area. Are you, Robert?"

Wilson leaned down to Fain, grabbed his collar and jerked him up off the floor in one swift motion. "Who is this dame? Are you responsible for her being here?

Fain straightened his coat back in place and made unintelligible protests. Flora spoke up and answered the question, "No, I can assure you, he is not. I am a representative of *The Houston Chronicle*, and I am here to interview you about the Tin and Sheet Metal Workers' strike that's going on."

Fain quickly voiced a disclaimer. "Oh, no, she's not. She's no newspaper writer. She's Fred Logan's daughter, and if she's here, it's to cause trouble. Because that's what she does best, in fact that's all she does. You better trust me on this one, Mr. Wilson."

Flora decided this would be a good time for her to leave and began edging toward the main entrance at her left, when suddenly everyone's attention was drawn to terrible noises coming from the elevator shaft at the rear of the lobby. The shaft reverberated with loud thuds and bams as if something was falling from the rooftop. Each thud caused an echo effect that finally ended with a muted thump as the object struck the bottom. Cries from the men above broke the silence, as workers yelled into the shaft.

Flora ran over with the group of men who had been challenging her, but she was sorry that she did so. At the bottom of the elevator shaft, resting on the soggy sand bed, lay a man who was a mass of limp, bruised limbs. A wretched, misshapen form, a lifeless body. Flora looked at the stranger lying there dead and a chill went through her. Her stomach recoiled as if she had been punched, and she realized this death could signify a malevolence far greater than she had visualized.

Wilson acted quickly, signaling two men. They jerked a piece of gray canvas from the floor, covered the body, and slid a plank under him, carrying the man through the front entry. The remaining men took off their caps and bowed their heads as the body passed. Flora studied the floor and her boots with grave deliberation, trying to figure out how she could tactfully leave.

To her right were five or six workmen whose mutterings were becoming louder. Grim-faced, one of them spoke, "That's number two! What do you expect when you name a hotel after a man that's been murdered in his sleep? The job's jinxed. I been saying it. I been telling all of you. Now maybe you'll believe me."

"Now, now, Mr. Joseph, this job's not jinxed. We're building the tallest building in Houston, maybe in the whole state, for all I know." Robert Wilson spoke loudly, knowing that the man's concerns were shared by other workers. "There's always going to be a few problems. Just a few problems, that's all." Wilson stretched out his arms in a familial gesture. "Does anyone know who this man was? Yell at the guys on top to come down and tell us what happened. Someone go outside and find a policeman. We're gonna have to report this."

Flora started for the door. She hastily crossed the lobby, keeping her head bowed so as not to attract attention, and for this reason slammed into Max Andrews. The collision knocked the breath out of her, but when she looked up and saw who it was, she gasped in relief, feeling he was again coming to her rescue. She smiled up at him tremulously and thought thank God, he is here and can deal with this disaster. She opened her mouth to explain what had happened, but Max cut her off.

"What in Sam Hill are you doing here?" He glared at her and continued shouting without giving her time to answer. "I just got a telephone call telling me about a death here on the job site. How did you find out about it?" She gasped, but before she could speak, he fired another question. "Do you ever stay where you are supposed to stay, or do what you're supposed to do?" He grabbed her arm and shook it. "Don't you have any sense of propriety?"

His attack was much too much like the tirade she'd just listened to from a man she despised, and though she certainly did not despise Max Andrews, her anger and outrage at being misjudged boiled over.

"Mr. Andrews, I'm sorry that I have not sat at home and waited for the men in my life to solve the serious problems with which I have been faced during the past week." She reached down and straightened her skirt. "I intended to go to my china painting class at Levy Brothers this morning, but it seemed like it would be such a lark to come here and meet all of these nice gentlemen." Flora glared first at Andrews and then at the astonished group of rowdies surrounding the foreman. "Now one of them is dead, and there's yet another problem. Do you think you can handle this one as promptly and efficiently as you've handled the others?" Flora paused and looked up at Andrews challengingly.

"While we're on the subject of my obstreperous behavior, let me introduce you to someone who knows exactly how you feel." She turned and walked toward Ward Fain who was standing nearby, his rabbity ears twitching, his bald head covered with sweat. "Mr. Andrews, I want you to meet Ward Fain, my father's manager at the marble yard. Go on, you two must talk, you have so much in common."

Flora turned back to Max Andrews, who was studying her in amazement. Then she fluttered her hand as if dismissing them and bid the assembled group of men goodbye as she stomped out the door.

Wilson spoke first, "Fain, go after her."

Ward whispered loudly, "No, not now."

Max Andrews walked closer to Ward Fain. "My name is Max Andrews, and I need to question you with regard to the allocation of operating funds at Logan's Marble Yard. I'm probating Fred Logan's will, and you'll need to furnish me with a set of the books. You are the bookkeeper, I presume."

"Yessir, yessir. You just come by anytime. They're ready." Ward wiped his sweaty mouth with his forefinger. "But Mr. Andrews, I need to explain about what Miss Flora said. She really is a ridiculous, headstrong, impulsive woman who has no business. . ."

"Mr. Fain, I am not going to discuss Miss Logan with you. I assure you that her actions are seldom a surprise to me."

"Well, if that's the case, you are a whole lot more unflappable than I am. She just beats all as far as I'm concerned."

"Mr. Fain, I said I don't want to discuss Miss Logan." Then he turned toward Robert Wilson and said, "What I do want to discuss, as Mr. Jesse Jones' legal counsel, are the circumstances which have resulted in a death on this job site. Who was the man that fell to his death, and how did this *accident* occur?"

CHAPTER ELEVEN

D usk settled as Flora sat in the white wicker swing sur-
veying Harvard Street from her front porch. Her feet
tapped the wooden boards relentlessly as she pushed herself to and fro. Each time she thumped the porch floor with her
boots, she thought of Max Andrews. She considered herself
strong and fearless, but the day's events had devastated her.
How could this have happened? Not only had she muffed her
chance to get the journal back, she had made a fool of herself in
front of her worst enemy and her new friend.

In her lap lay the evening newspaper. She had read and
reread the sensational headlines and the accompanying story.
The man who had tragically fallen to his death that morning
had been a Mr. Chandler Parker, thirty-three years old and a
newcomer to Houston. Today had been his first day on the Rice
Hotel job. Witnesses saw him stumble over a coil of rope and
plunge down the elevator shaft. The coroner stated that the man
was probably killed before he had fallen twelve stories, having
been dashed from side to side of the shaft, striking heavy beams
and planks as he fell. The paper stated he'd come to Houston
because he thought the climate would be beneficial for his invalid wife. She told the police that her husband had been a
carpenter and a railroad fireman, but had given up those jobs
because of poor eyesight. The paper listed his address as 1616
Franklin Avenue and announced that an inquest would be held
in Judge Crooker's court. They called it the longest fall in the
history of skyscraper fatalities.

Flora twisted her hands. Reading about the accident was
almost as upsetting as witnessing it. When the death occurred,
she was so shocked she'd hardly reacted to Mr.Parker's tragedy.
Her focus had been on the men she stood in front of and her
fear that they had murdered again. When Max Andrews arrived,
her intense relief was destroyed by his first words. She shook
when she thought about what had happened and felt a deep
sadness for this poor woman and her late husband, the hopes
they must have had, the expectations of sharing in the prosper-
ity of this city. What had led the unfortunate Mr. Parker to the
Rice Hotel? What had led her there today? As horrible as the

experience had been, she had gained information from the visit. She now knew who had stolen her father's journal, and she had proof that Fain was in cahoots with the crooked foreman.

She stopped the swing abruptly with both feet, realizing she must go to his widow, express her sympathy, and ask why her husband had chosen to come to Houston. Sleep eluded her that night. After tossing among her bed covers for several hours, she dropped off only to awaken with a scream.

Her dream was of the death she had seen that day; she kept hearing the whamming of the body as it plummeted down the eighteen stories. When she went over to look at the body, the corpse was her father instead of the stranger. Dawn came, and she rose groggy and sluggish, slipping into her wrapper and stumbling to the washstand where she poured water into the porcelain basin and cupped her hands to splash some on her swollen eyes. She surveyed herself in the mirror and grimaced.

She finished a hasty toilette, threw on a waist and skirt, pulled her boots from under the bed and began the tedious lacing. As she poked the cotton laces from eyelet to eyelet, she planned what she would do. It is important that I question Mrs. Parker, because I know about the dirty dealings on the job site. Perhaps, her husband knew something he should not have. She would ask the widow if Mr. Parker had gotten wind of the graft being practiced on the job? Most important, she needed to know if his death was connected with her father's?

She owed it to Mrs. Parker as well as to her own family to find out, and she could do a better job of questioning the widow than the police. She knew what questions to ask and she knew how to ask them so that the woman was not treated shabbily or unkindly. "I must do this," she announced emphatically as she whacked her hairbrush down the length of her copper-colored mane. Annie glanced up from a pan of apples as Flora came in the kitchen. Flora gave her a sadfaced look and flounced over to the stove. She poured her coffee and sat down at the table with an "ugh."

"Miz Flora, what's the matter? Is that too strong?"

"No, Annie, the coffee's fine, but I'm not. I can't stop worrying about that poor widow whose husband fell to his death.

103

"I expect there's not many victuals in her cupboard. I could fill a basket with some tins, and you could get Caleb to take it to her. Canned goods that'll keep. Maybe you could pick her out some clothes. Did the paper say what size she is?" Annie held up her hands as if measuring what she thought the widow would be. "Didn't the paper say she was kinda poorly? She's probably your mama's size." Annie continued despite Flora's silence. "Some of your mama's dresses are just up there mildewing. Maybe the lady could use a shawl or a wrapper."

Flora looked at her contritely. "Yes, Annie, that's an excellent idea. I think she would qualify as 'poorly' indeed. Put together some food for her and I'll look through Mother's things."

They soon had a hamper ready full of assorted footstuffs and clothing. Flora had chosen a flannelette nightgown, a black striped wool cape, and a pink knitted shawl from her mother's clothes.

"Mis Flora, you can't carry this stuff to Franklin Street by yoreself. I'm coming with you; and just don't say 'no'."

Flora looked at Annie standing beside her in the hallway, and tears came to her eyes at the woman's kindliness and sensitivity to this stranger's misfortune.

The ringing of the telephone interrupted. Flora went to the hall table and lifted the receiver. She mouthed "Dessie" to Annie and answered her friend. "Yes, I was about to go downtown. Come over and go with me to run a quick errand just a few blocks past the courthouse and then we can shop." She nodded her head at Dessie's reply. "Okay, if you're sure he wouldn't mind. I'll be watching for the car."

Flora hung up and turned back to Annie. "Dessie's going with me, and Mr. Stanley's taking us in the Ford. This is better than trying to lug the stuff on the trolley."

"What's Miss Dessie gonna say about your going to see Miz Parker? Does she know you seed that man dead?"

"Oh, Annie, I'll explain everything to Dessie. She'll know I did the right thing. She never criticizes me anyway. " While Flora was convinced of the importance of her trip to the widow, she wondered what Mr. Andrews would think? Would he call her more names? Would he think her meddlesome? Or would he understand?

In less than twenty minutes the girls were motoring to town with Carter. When Dessie began questioning Flora about her errand and the basket Annie helped her load into the back seat, Flora rolled her eyes and put her forefinger to her lips. Dessie nodded, and the two young women chatted about tulle and lace, and the importance of ordering white roses in advance.

Flora gave Carter the address listed in the paper. "I appreciate this, Mr. Stanley. The Sunshine Society found out about this poor woman's plight, and since I was going through Mother's clothes, I offered to bring the basket. I didn't realize it was so far. I'm glad I didn't have to walk all this way."

"Miss Logan, you'd never have made it. Why don't you make me a batch of fudge to show your appreciation?"

Seeing Flora's look of dismay, Carter hastily withdrew the request. The three story wooden dwelling Flora sought displayed the numbers 1616 boldly painted in white on a handsome dark green sign that looked like it was worth more than the house. Under the numerals was printed with equal boldness "Mrs. Rosa Thomson's Boarding House," and in smaller letters the invitation to "inquire within."

Flora and Dessie went up the steps and stood on the unpainted porch, waiting for someone to answer the bell. A snaggle-toothed woman opened the sagging screen door and peered at them suspiciously.

"You want a room?" She looked them over, taking in their straw bonnets, simple clothing and the hamper Flora carried. "You girls just get to town? What'd you do, leave the farm? Yeah, yeah, everybody's coming to Houston. Looking for a job, I bet. Well, you two've come to the right place. Every restaurant in town's looking for help. You'll find work waiting on tables in no time."

Flora spoke before the woman had a chance to say more. "We're here to see Mrs.Chandler Parker. We've brought her some food and clothing. May we come in, please?"

The woman turned her head, and her black eyes snapped open and shut like Flora's old baby doll. Wiry gray curls protruded from her faded red turban. She wore large circle earrings of tarnished gold. Her swarthy skin was paper thin and creased with lines.

"Oh! I guess so." Her eyes opened wide. "I had you pegged for honest working girls, not fancy do-good-ers. Don't know what'll happen to that woman, I sure don't. She's lucky her husband paid for the week in advance. I'd, of course, hate to do it, but I'd have to ask her to leave. I mean, you can understand, this is a business." She smacked her lips as if tasting something good. "It's all I have to support myself since my Jim went to his grave, God rest his soul. What's this town coming to? Poor lady losing her husband so quick like. They'd only just come. Did you read about it in the *Post?* I guess everyone'll be wanting to see her. She's famous now." Mrs. Rosa Thomson paused briefly, but it was long enough for Flora to interrupt her garrulous outpouring.

"Mrs. Thomson, we came to see Mrs. Parker. Will you direct us to her room, please?"

"Guess you can't just pass the time in a friendly way. You society ladies are all the same. Here I was trying to acquaint you with my boarding house and tell you how long the Parkers had been here, and you cut me off as if you don't have time for the likes of me. Yeah, I know your type."

"Mrs. Thomson, I meant no insult. I must see Mrs. Parker and talk with her. Please, understand."

"What you got in that basket? You bringing that stuff to her? Ha! Boy are you in for a surprise. Well, her room's on the third floor, first door on your right."

Flora looked at Dessie and raised her eyebrows questioningly then shrugged her shoulders and led the way.

"Watch those stairs at the top. They're pretty steep." The landlady started up behind them. "Mr. Thomson, that was my beloved husband who's gone to meet his maker, always was going to fix them so they'd be right. He said again and again, 'Rosa, I promise you if it's the last thing I do, I'll rebuild those stairs." She stopped abruptly and lowered her voice, continuing in a whining whisper. " It weren't the last thing he did! The last thing he did was to visit the privy over there in the side yard, and that's where it happened."

"What happened, Mrs. Thomson?" Flora asked curiously.

"He died! I always did say one of these days, a man's gonna die there cause that's where they spend the most time."

Flora and Dessie gasped in horror, unable to hide their shock.

"Oh, I'm sorry, Miss. I didn't mean to offend you. Ladies like you don't talk about things like that, do you?"

Flora struggled to speak. Finally, she said weakly, "Mrs. Thomson, that's okay, but if you don't mind, we're going on up now. In case we don't see you before we leave, it's been a pleasure to meet you."

"Oh don't worry about that, dearie, I'll be right here when you come down. I'm gonna see how you like Widow Parker."

The girls turned back and cautiously made their way up the steep passage. When they reached the third floor landing, Dessie halted and challenged her friend, "Why are we up here? You haven't told me a thing." Her voice quivered. "We've come all this way. What's the secret? What have you done now?"

Briefly, Flora told of seeing Mr. Parker's fall. Dessie's blue eyes widened, and much to Flora's disgust she started fanning herself with her hand. Flora turned on her heel, walked to the widow's door, and knocked softly. She waited several minutes without getting a response.

"Flora, she's not home. We'd better just leave the basket. She's probably gone to town."

"The paper said she's an invalid. I don't think she's away. I'll knock once more." She rapped on the door louder.

"Yes," a thin querulous voice answered, "who is it?"

"Mrs. Parker, we've come from the Sunshine Society in Houston Heights. We have food and clothing for you." Flora spoke earnestly.

The door flew open as if the occupant had stood behind it listening. The widow was not what Flora expected. She was large with a full face, red cheeks and a rounded chin which spread down her throat. Her eyes were piercingly green, and she peered at them with much the same suspicion they'd encountered below. Flora was beginning to question her charitable effort. The woman clutched her worn pink satin wrapper across her bosom and stared at the basket, sniffing the air expectantly.

"What you got there? Must be canned stuff, don't have no smell." She turned her back on her visitors, walked to the window and sat down heavily in a large threadbare club chair the arms and back of which were dressed with dingy pink doilies.

"My father's company is associated with the construction of the Rice Hotel, and I was there the day your husband passed away."

"Passed away! You mean throwed away! His life was throwed away, and for what? A fancy hotel for rich folks to live it up, folks that don't have bills to pay like you and me." The widow's chest heaved with indignation, and she leaned forward and thrust an angry fist two inches from Flora's face.

She ducked instinctively though the woman came no closer. "Mrs. Parker, we're so sorry about your husband's unfortunate accident. I understand you've been in Houston only a short while. Didn't you come here from Alabama?"

"Left those pretty rolling hills for this flatland. It's a crying shame. Always looking for greener grass; that was Chandler Parker. As soon as that letter came from Cousin Rita, he couldn't talk of nothing but Houston. Said he wanted to find a better climate, a place where I could get well. People talk about this being a bustling boom town, but it's a mosquito-filled swamp to me. There's nothing healthy about this place." She paused, rummaged in her pocket and brought out a grimy, yellow-flowered handkerchief. She proceeded to cough loudly, holding the kerchief to her mouth. "I sit here and look out this window at this road, filled day and night with wagons hauling goods back and forth. If I raise the window, I'm choked by dust, bitten by bugs, and deafened by the yells of drunks staggering out of the saloons on both corners." She paused again and blew her nose loudly. "A dirty stinking hell hole, hemmed in by dirty stinking bayous. Might be a bunch of men think this is a boomtown, but not many women would agree."

"But Mrs. Parker, your husband felt he had a wonderful opportunity here, didn't he?" Mrs. Parker remained stonily silent. "Did you say you have a cousin in Houston? Did she help him get the job?" Flora asked.

"Yes, he has a cousin here all right. Miss Rita Campbell. She works over off Washington Avenue, and knows lots of men that were working on the Rice Hotel job. She got him that job with the Otis Elevator Company, but she hasn't so much as paid me a visit since Mr. Parker's accident. Yeah, that Rita knows a lot of men."

Flora held her breath to keep from exclaiming. She exhaled carefully and then spoke, "Mrs. Parker, did your husband ever mention a man by the name of Ward Fain?"

"No, not as I recall. Is he a friend of Rita's?"

"Yes, they're very good friends. I thought she might've told you about him in the letter you said she wrote." The widow shook her head no. Flora tried again. "Did Mr. Parker meet the foreman on the job? A man named Robert Wilson."

"Who knows? I don't, that's for sure. I don't think he met him till he got here to start working. Last time I seed him alive was when he set off for work. Carried his lunchpail. I can still see him trudging down Franklin Avenue. Didn't know he was walking to his death. Didn't know. Very last time. Never again. If only we hadn't come here." She hung her head and studied the thin gold ring on her left hand.

"What'd you girls say you brought in that basket? What kind of food? Any candy?"

"No, we didn't think to bring candy. But here's some canned milk. You could make some pralines or fudge."

"Well, I guess I could, if I could stand over that gas burner and stir it in a pan for thirty minutes." She whined accusingly. "Oh well, I know you didn't come to listen to my troubles. I've never had a well day, and that's a fact. What else is there?"

"Here's a glass of plum preserves and wrapped up in this waxed paper are three biscuits from this morning. Here's a jar of green tomato pickles and a glass of currant conserve. Oh, this is a slice of molasses cake made this last week. I know you'll like it." Flora felt like a peddler trying to sell wares. She looked at the woman sprawled in the chair, fanning herself with a newspaper, her loose wrapper gaping open revealing more rolls of fat.

"Just leave the stuff on the counter. No, bring me those biscuits and that piece of cake, Dearie. I'll go through the canned stuff when I feel better." Her chin bobbled as she reached for the food Flora held out to her. Suddenly loud shrieks were heard from the street. Mrs. Parker stood and leaned out the window. She squinted her eyes as she looked down below and let out a cackle.

109

"Lookee there, that drunk fell down in the road. He's laying there, can't even move. You girls belong to the WCTU? I bet you do. You look the type for it. You could go down and convert him." She laughed at her cleverness and looked sideways at Flora and Dessie. "What's a poor woman to do? Just have to sit here and wait for my cousin Willie and her husband. Got a yellow message they're on their way here."

Her visitors edged toward the door, "Goodbye, Mrs. Parker, hope you enjoy the food." Flora pulled the door shut and scrambled down the stairs two at a time, Dessie in tow. Before they got to the bottom, they could see Mrs. Thomson, grinning up at them just as she had promised.

"And how did you find the poor grieving widow? Did she like the food? Doesn't seem about to waste away, does she? Her cousin is supposed to arrive soon and take her back to Birmingham."

"Good day, Madam." Flora and Dessie left just as fast as they could get out of the house. They walked in silence until they were in front of the courthouse.

"I have never seen anything as bad as her in all my life." Dessie announced.

"Chandler Parker could have leaped down that hole. I'm not sure I wouldn't have. What if you had to come home to that every night? She's awful, and so's the landlady!" Flora grimaced. The only information she had gotten was that she needed to look more closely at Rita Campbell. How interesting that Logan's employee had persuaded the elevator company to hire an ex-carpenter/fireman who had poor eyesight. As Aunt Ruth was prone to say, "I don't understand all I know."

"What don't you understand, Flora?" Dessie asked.

"Oh nothing. I wish I could feel that we had comforted Mr. Parker's widow, but I don't think the woman could be comforted by anything except maybe candy."

They were crossing Fannin when Dessie nudged Flora in the ribs. "There's your beau!"

Flora looked up and ducked her head, glad for the wide brim of her hat. She began walking faster and Dessie fussed beside her. "He's all the way across the street, and he probably won't even notice us; especially if you slow down to a normal pace. You're moving like a runaway horse."

Flora slowed but kept her head lowered, carefully watching the pavement. She failed to see Dessie wave her arm vigorously in the air.

"Here he comes. Why're you so upset? I thought you liked him," Dessie questioned. "He escorted you home from the club meeting. What's the matter? Oh, never mind, here he is."

"Hello, Mr. Andrews. How are you today?" Dessie smiled cordially, and Flora gritted her teeth.

"Hello, Miss Trichelle and Miss Logan. Are you in town for some shopping?" He removed his hat politely and then put it back on. "Or have you come to give the 11:00 deposition we had set up for the day I saw you at the Rice Hotel?" Flora remained mulishly silent but raised her eyes and glared at him then studied the pavement below her feet. "Maybe you came for the lunch date we made for that same day?" She could feel his stare boring into the the crown of her hat, as he waited for her to look at him. She kept studying her boots. "Miss Logan has a poor memory, Miss Trichelle, but since you've been friends for so long I am sure you have experienced her forgetfulness."

"No, I don't know anything of the kind; in fact she's . . ." said Dessie, obviously launching into a defensive.

"Mr. Andrews, stop it. She knows nothing about this. She doesn't realize that you are being facetious." Flora looked up at him, her eyes dark with anger, her words like shards of glass. They stared at each other. Flora lowered her head so he would not see how he had hurt her.

"Miss Logan, I'm sorry for what I said yesterday. I didn't mean to criticize your actions. You have a right to go where you want, but I feared for your safety." Dessie gasped, but they both ignored her. "Those men were very angry with you, and I didn't know where their anger was leading." Max Andrews reached toward her, put one hand in the crook of her elbow, and with his other hand tilted the brim of her hat upward. She raised her face towards him, but her look was defiant, not penitent. She could not tell if he caught her message, but he studied her eyes as if he were looking into her soul. She felt naked before his scrutiny and began pinching the folds of her skirt.

"Mr. Andrews, where should we go from here?"

111

He wrinkled his brow and looked uncertain, taken aback by the bold honesty of her question. His face reddened, and he turned to Dessie, still holding Flora's arm close to his side. "Miss Trichelle, may I escort you ladies to lunch? The White Kitchen is up in the next block. I eat there often and can recommend the food."

Dessie grinned and looked at the two of them. "That's a fine idea, Mr. Andrews. I am all in, and besides I don't think I could walk much further without a rest." She smiled happily. "I would be happy to accompany the two of you; if fact, I feel it is my duty, though I'm not sure whether I'll be a referee or a chaperon."

Flora refused to be baited by her friend. As soon as they were seated in the restaurant and had given their order to the waiter, Flora blurted out, "You might as well know right now, I have been to visit Chandler Parker's widow."

"What made you think that was necessary?" Max asked curiously.

"I wanted to know if she might have heard her husband speak of any problems on the job." She looked at him, trying to gauge his reaction. "But it was his first day at work, and she never saw him again after he left home that morning." Flora shook her head sadly. "I also wondered why he came to Houston. I did find out the answer to that question, but I can't figure how the two pieces fit together. I doubt he was in cahoots with the foreman and his gang. He hadn't been here long enough."

"Mr. Jones has had investigators checking the same thing. They found no reason to suspect Mr. Parker's death was anything other than a tragic accident. I wish you had not witnessed it. I think you should leave it be, Flora. You've been through enough."

"Why? Because I am a member of the 'weaker' sex and might have fainted at the sight of blood, or was it for the same reason I would not have wanted you or Dessie to see what happened? It was an ugly thing for anyone to see, regardless of their sex."

"You're right, and I'm wrong. I apologize for trying to protect you and wrap you in cotton. You deserve more than that. Will you forgive me?" Max spoke softly, his eyes searching her face. She looked up at him and grinned crookedly.

"That's a first," she answered ruefully.

"What do you mean? he asked.

"An apology from a man. A man who admits that he is wrong about something. Thank you, Mr. Andrews. I accept your apology."

Dessie, silent during their conversation, now spoke briskly, "Flora, try some of your oyster shortcake. Mine is delicious. How is your Spanish hash, Mr. Andrews?"

With this, the mood swung to a lighter note and the ladies described what shopping they had planned for the afternoon. They parted from Andrews outside the restaurant with Flora promising to come Saturday morning to give the deposition.

As the ladies headed for Levy Brothers, they chatted about everything except Max Andrews, and Flora was grateful Dessie sensed it was not a subject she was ready to discuss.

CHAPTER TWELVE

Church bells pealed as Flora came down the front steps. Caleb waited in the buggy. He was smiling, and Flora was relieved. When she had told him that without the journal it would be hard to prove the graft, Caleb nonchalantly replied, "Flo, you and I read the journal. We know Papa wasn't part of the underhanded dealings going on at the Rice. That's all that matters."

She climbed into the buggy and like a dog with a bone, started back on the possibility of Ward Fain or Robert Wilson having murdered their father. Caleb listened and then replied stubbornly, "You say Mr. Jones has a private investigator checking into what Papa wrote in the journal. That's enough for me. I don't want you going around these men anymore." Flora bit her lip to keep from replying to his irritatingly avuncular tone. "They aren't worth the powder it'd take to blow them up. Leave it be."

Flora was silent as she decided how far to question his desire to drop the subject. What had caused his sudden change of heart? Did he fear Ward Fain would be the guilty party and that Logan's would lose its manager? Surely, Caleb was not letting business concerns influence him regarding Fred Logan's death. Why had he insisted she come home if he wanted to let things stay as they were? Did he think like the trolley conductor, "Dead is Dead"? She feared his continuing to work with Fain, but had no evidence to support her fears. She should have told him right away who Fain was and what he had done, but she hadn't, and the longer she waited, the worse the situation became and the guiltier she felt.

"Caleb, is that all you wanted to know?" Flora pulled his sleeve and forced him to look at her, "whether Papa was part of the Rice Hotel payoff?" He averted his eyes and ducked his head. "You thought he was, didn't you? You knew this was going on." He turned, and she could see his sad face. Were his so-called suspicions regarding Fred Logan's death only a ploy to gain her assistance in uncovering the corruption? "You don't think Papa was murdered? What did you want from me?"

"I don't know why I wanted you to come, but I guess I thought you could straighten it all out." He shrugged his shoulders. "When this Mr. Parker fell to his death, I decided it wasn't for us to find the answers." Flora felt a frustration greater than anything she had known.

"Don't look at me like that," Caleb said.

"I'll look at you any way I please," Flora responded and shifted to another sore point. "What about Rita Campbell? Did you know she was a cousin of the man who fell down the elevator shaft? What do you know about her?"

Caleb pulled a piece of lint off the sleeve of his dark blue jacket and concentrated on his mare's hooves hitting the brick pavement.

"Do you trust Rita? Maybe she's Robert Wilson's girlfriend." He turned red as a radish but made no comment.

"Caleb, are you smitten by her?" There, it was out. She had wanted to ask him since the first week she came. She held her breath, waiting for him to answer.

"Could be," he answered nonchalantly.

"What does that mean?" Flora cocked her head sideways and studied him, trying to conceal her dismay.

"Well, she's sorta playing the field right now. She's still grieving over Papa. You know, you weren't nice to her that day y'all met. She told me how you acted."

"I'm sorry. I was surprised to see a woman like her working at the marble yard. Maybe I misjudged her. I'll run by there tomorrow and apologize, how about that?" Was there no limit to male foolishness?

"Thanks, sis. That would really make me happy."

"Caleb, since you're so pleased at having her there, I wondered what you would think if I worked there too?"

Caleb pulled halted the buggy and looked at her incredulously. "I don't think so. You'd just be in the way. You don't know how to deal with the grinders, the stonecutters and the suppliers. That's rough work, not a job for a lady."

"Excuse me, what's a good job for a lady?"

"Oh, Florie, come on, you know what ladies are supposed to do. If they don't get hitched, then they have to be schoolteachers or music teachers or something like that." He hemmed and hawed for half a block and then said, "They sure don't run a marble yard."

"Why not? Max Andrews and Jesse Jones think it's a good idea." Flora rejoined boldly.

"Gosh, I don't know why." Caleb looked at her in surprise. Apparently, the idea had never occurred to him. "What would Rita and Ward say?"

"What in heaven's name does that have to do with anything?" Flora couldn't believe her ears. "I don't care what that woman thinks about anything, if she even has a brain to think . . ." Flora stopped midsentence suddenly feeling uncertain in her low assessment of Rita's ability.

Caleb didn't notice she had stopped talking. As she looked at his spooney expression, she felt that he had tuned her out and was off in a dream world. Now she knew who he was dreaming of, and she wanted to shake him for not recognizing Rita as an opportunist who had first ensnared the father, and then the son. She realized with a sinking heart that if Rita wanted Caleb, he was hers for the taking. She also realized that as long as he was under this woman's spell, he couldn't be a partner or an ally. She stared at the quiet tree-lined esplanade and wished she were back in New York City. Caleb had always been immature and insecure. Orphaned at five, he spent two years being

115

passed from relative to relative before coming to the Logans. Though her parents had provided a foster home with material comforts, she knew he had never gotten the kind of emotional support he must have craved. Growing up with him, Flora was ashamed to say she never gave him much thought except as a pesky younger brother who was easily led into mischief by his imaginative, impulsive, older sister. She had never recognized what a shallow saucer he was, and that made her glad she hadn't tried to tell him about Fain.

Tomorrow she would pay another visit to the office and chat with Rita, maybe even take her to lunch. "I need a different kind of knowledge from that which Mr. Jones' investigator can uncover." Flora spoke under her breath as Caleb got out of the buggy and tied up to the post.

"I'm glad we're going to the new Episcopal mission. It's called St. Andrew's?" Flora spoke brightly, deciding to put aside her disappointment and enjoy the day.

"Yes, there's no church building yet. We worship here at Rev. Mr. and Mrs. Henry Brown's home."

"Who's having the picnic? Christ Church downtown? Was that where you went before St. Andrew's got started?"

"Yes, their picnic is the best of anyone's. They have over a thousand members, and they sure know how to have a party!"

"Well, I've heard Sylvan Beach is fun. This will be a wonderful day."

She admired Mr. Brown's gray two story house neatly trimmed in slate blue. A white picket fence marked off the front yard, the pavement flanked by flower beds filled with bronze chrysanthemums.

"Mrs. Brown must be quite a gardener. I went to school with Julia. Does she still live here?"

"Yes, she does. A sweeter girl than her, I've never known. And boy does she make dandy fudge! Sometimes, I come over in the evening, and we play high five or peanut jab."

Flora decided that this was definitely a relationship which needed developing. They reached the front porch and rang the bell which was answered by the young woman of whom Caleb had spoken. "Ah, here is the fair Miss Brown. You remember Flora, don't you?"

The girl standing in front of them was everything Flora was not, a young woman who behaved perfectly. Caleb called her "sweet." That sounded like she was just as boring as she used to be, but next to Rita, Julia seemed an outstanding choice for Caleb. Flora held out her hand and smiled warmly.

"Of course I do. It's a pleasure to see you again, Julia."

"You look different, so ladylike." Julia carefully appraised her. Flora smoothed her white duck skirt and bit her tongue. "What a wonderful outfit. Did that come from New York City? Caleb keeps us informed of all of your activities. He's so proud of you."

Flora blushed and turned to Caleb who was beaming with pride. She looked down and rubbed the lapels of her jacket with its bold green and white vertical stripes. Nothing like this would be available in Houston for two or three years. She felt she looked her best. Her large white straw bowler trimmed with a dark green grosgrain band had a picnic look about it and was on sale because it was out of season.

Julia led them into the parlor where the service was conducted. Flora was impressed with Mrs. Brown's decor. The wallpaper was embossed with velvet, but the blue and rose colors were softer than the dreary burgundy so often used. The crown molding was golden oak as were the baseboards and window frames, and the glass panes were covered with filmy lace. The fireplace on the north wall with its heavily carved mantel was an interesting focal point. Matching fern stands with barley twist legs flanked the hearth. On each were large china jardinieres decorated with pink roses. Maybe Julia had learned to paint china. That sounded like something she would enjoy. A refectory table had been placed in front of the fireplace and was dressed with altar hangings and a two foot simple wooden cross. Some wooden chairs were lined up in front of the makeshift altar.

Mrs. Brown sat down at the parlor organ in the corner and played softly at first and then louder as others arrived and sat down. She stopped the music when Reverend Mr. Brown, wearing a black cassock and narrow white tippet, came out of the kitchen door, through the dining room and into the parlor. He was preceded by a young acolyte dressed in a long black

117

cassock and snowy surplice. Mr. Brown turned to face the group and began the Morning Prayer service which filled the room like a favorite poem. For the sermon hymn, they joyfully sang four verses of *All Things Bright and Beautiful.* Mr. Brown's text was from the Book of John, and he startled Flora with his opening line.

"Will ye also go away?" As he continued, his words seemed to refer to her life: her fears, her regrets, and her concerns. He admonished the congregation saying, "You will never see the ripened fruit of the vine, hanging in clustered fatness unless the invisible sap is coursing from the lifegiving root." He made her think about the rootlessness with which she was struggling. Mr. Brown continued, "Nor is the sap rising to any matured purpose, unless it produces the flower and the fruitage of abundance." Flora wondered where her life was going? Was the New York Botanical Gardens the place for her? A successor, perhaps, to the directress Elizabeth Britton? Or was her place here in Houston Heights? She felt like what the minister called "a boat propelled by a single oar, going around in circles without any progress."

He ended with a final charge to his congregation, "Go somewhere, *be* something, and *do* something. Misery, crime, poverty, and vice are increasing while you are sleeping. Oh, my brethren, will ye also go away?"

Deeply moved, she stood with the group and sang the familiar hymn *Come Labor On.* Mrs. Brown let out all the stops on the final verse, and the members responded by singing vigorously.

Flora paid little attention to the close of the service or the chatter among the group of worshipers. She was lost in thoughts of New York City, and the home she had come back to. Could she go away? Could she do as Caleb asked and forget about the mystery which surrounded her father's death and her suspicions of Ward Fain? No. Every fiber in her body rejected this course of action. She had to be true to herself and her feelings.

"Flora, Julia has consented to go on the picnic with us." Her thoughts were interrupted by Caleb's pleased announcement.

"That's wonderful. We'll have a chance for a real visit, won't we, Julia?" She was delighted for anything that would distract Caleb from Rita Campbell.

She sensed someone standing behind her and turned to find another high school classmate. "Rufus Reed, isn't it?"

"You're right on the money, Florie." He looked at her and purposely crossed his eyes.

She winced at his use of the nickname she despised. Yes, she did remember Rufus. The only other redhead in their class, a fact which had occasioned many jokes.

"I don't do that any more except for old time's sake. How's 'my little gypsy sweetheart' as the song says?"

"Rufus, you must be thinking of someone else. We were never sweethearts!" Flora responded indignantly.

"Can't blame a fellow for trying, can you? You were always A-number-one in my book." Rufus guffawed noisily and grinned at her; she laughed in spite of herself. She had forgotten what a cutup he always was.

"Say, your cousin invited me to join the group going to Sylvan Beach. Have they rented railroad cars from the LaPorte line?"

Flora nodded her head, scarcely believing that her "wonderful" day was now going to be spent with these high school chums. She laughed to herself at this respite from her sleuthing, if her actions could be considered such, and managed to smile as she joined arms with Rufus and Caleb. With Julia hanging on to Caleb, the foursome proceeded out to the buggy.

Caleb drove home, and they alit as he unharnessed Lucy and led her to the barn. Riding the trolley downtown, they got off at the depot where the Houston, LaPorte, and Northern Line started. A crowd of picnickers waited in line, the men all wearing light-colored suits and panamas, the ladies in white cotton dresses and broad-brimmed leghorns. It would be the last picnic of the year and everyone noisily exchanged greetings with friends, glad to extend the summer's fun into fall. Though Flora did not know the group, she enjoyed the camaraderie.

The train pulled in, and they swarmed aboard with their hampers, pasteboard boxes, and satchels containing the picnic dinners for the day. Smells of fried chicken, stuffed eggs, and potato salad wafted through the railroad car. A young man named

119

Mr. Wilkes had brought an accordion. He began with "Wait till the Sun Shines, Nellie," and everyone chimed in. In the hour it took to reach the beach, they ran through all the popular songs from the syrupy sentimental "End of a Perfect Day" to "Take Me Out to the Ball Game." Not since Flora left Houston for New York had she been part of a group like this, and she realized how much she had missed the sense of community New York City could never provide.

As she rode along the flat countryside, browned from the harsh summer sun and barren except for the scrub oaks and palmettos, she admitted to herself that coming back to Houston had brought something else to her life that she had neither sought nor expected. Her meeting with Max Andrews yesterday was still on her mind.

She had gone to his office to give the deposition and identify Mr. Walters as the man she now thought had stolen the journal. Afterwards they discussed details of the case against Robert Wilson, the assumed "R.W." mentioned in the journal. Max felt her father's intent to expose R.W. might have resulted in his death. They were in agreement that the death was a murder rather than a suicide.

She tried not to seem vague when he asked if there were other entries. Max assured her he would have the investigator check out Walters as well as Wilson. Max regarded Wilson as a suspect since he had the most to lose if Logan had decided on exposure of the corruption. He felt it unlikely the foreman committed the murder himself, but he could have directed an underling to do it and not batted an eye. The fact that the death of Fred Logan was not even considered a murder by the police, indicated how clever he had been.

Flora knew whom she suspected and with great reluctance she revealed her Big Thicket experience with Ward Fain. Andrews listened without comment. She watched him, sitting behind his large oak desk, his elbows propped on the polished surface, his large fingers steepled, his blue eyes calm and cool.

"Did you hear what I said?" she asked embarrassed and humiliated by his silence.

"Of course I did. I heard about a courageous, headstrong, impulsive young girl who is not unlike the woman you've become." He sighed heavily. "I'm honored you've confided in me. I understand you better."

"Is that important? For you to understand me, I mean?"

"Yes, it is if we're to continue working together to solve this mystery."

Flora felt unaccountably disappointed by his answer. "What should be our next action, Mr. Andrews?" She reverted to a formality more appropriate for the business relationship Andrews seemed to be suggesting. She told him about Thurow's description of the person he had seen near the trolley track at dusk and her suspicions that the man could have been Fain in disguise.

Max nodded attentively. "We need to find out what Ward Fain's role has been. He must know about the graft? Did he profit from your father's death? Was he about to be fired as the diary hints? What's his game with Rita?" Max shot his questions like darts, and Flora could imagine him in a court of law impaling an opponent. "The agency I hired will find answers for most of this." Max had assessed the problem and seemed certain he would get results. He surprised her by saying, "I think I'll pay Mr. Fain a visit this evening. Maybe I can shake something out of him."

Flora agreed hesitatingly, wondering how far Max Andrews would go in questioning Fain. He sounded almost threatening. She stood to leave, and he came around his desk, looking down at her, his eyes now warm and inviting. She was startled when he reached down and wrapped her arm in his, holding her far closer than she'd have thought appropriate for a business partner.

"It's about lunchtime. Let's stop by Liberty's and get some sandwiches to go."

She looked at him questioningly. "Aren't we through? Is this a recess?"

"No, we're through. This is an outing, just for fun. Let's go down to the park, eat lunch and relax." Before she knew it, he was propelling her through the door.

Yesterday had been a fine October day, a crisp blue sky, little puffs of clouds and a hint of the fall that Houston never seemed to get. They'd sat together on a wooden bench gazing at the bandstand which she'd just discussed as she'd repeated her father's words describing the recent Fourth of July here at Sam Houston Park. After a leisurely lunch and debate over the merits of Houston's version of a New York deli sandwich, they climbed down to the wooden bridge which crossed the bayou. Buffalo Bayou was just a narrow stream at this point winding through the park. They threw bread crumbs to the loudly quacking ducks, and Flora wished for a camera so she could snap a picture of the palmettos and weeping willows that lined the banks of the water.

Max laughed as she spoke her wish, "Always the botanist."

"Yes, I guess you're right," she answered happily.

"What thoughts have you given to my suggestion?"

Flora pretended ignorance, not willing to indicate she had thought about it a lot.

"Will you stay here and take over your father's business?"

"I guess that decision will have to wait until I've found his murderer."

"I don't like your suggesting that *you* will find the murderer." Max answered brusquely. "Women's rights should never extend to their dealing with the criminal world. Of that I'm convinced."

"Oh, you are? How interesting! Did you know that a female has been commissioned as a police officer in Los Angeles, California?"

Max looked at her in astonishment. "Surely not."

"Yes, it's true. I read of her work last year in *Good Housekeeping*. She discussed the benefits for the city of having a woman in the police department."

Max shook his head ruefully. "I can't imagine what they would be. You ladies are coming to the forefront, but I'll wager we never see a woman employed as a police officer in Houston, Texas."

She could feel him staring at her and when she looked up, he spoke seriously, "Promise you won't seek out more danger. I appreciate your willingness to help and I applaud your courage, but . . ."

"Mr. Andrews, I don't wish to offend you, but you are a

hypocrite. You champion the rights of women, but you don't want us to use these rights. We should keep them packed away in a trunk at home, like souvenirs, taking them out only to admire them as we do our lace scarves and velvet roses."

Max was stung by her criticism; his face reddened and he clenched his pipe stem tightly. Flora continued, ignoring his glare.

"This lady police officer points the way. Where she leaves off, other women may begin. We can help to better social conditions, I know we can."

He stubbornly shook his head. "As always, Miss Logan, you provide much for me to think on. I did not realize my position lacked substance, but perhaps, you're right. I still must ask you to promise that you'll leave Ward Fain to me. You don't know what sort of grudge he may harbor, and you have no business trying to flush him out. I'll take care of him."

"There it is, there's the water." Her thoughts were interrupted by Rufus pointing south as the train rolled to a halt. The strip of hazy blue beckoned them in the distance. The boisterous group got off the train and walked toward the park. Soft Bermuda grass covered the meadow which sloped down to the water's edge. A welcome breeze ruffled the long swags of gray-green Spanish moss which hung from the stately oak trees. The tangy salt air and the sparkling bay before them were intoxicating, and Flora delighted in the landscape. Rufus ran on ahead and grabbed a table shaded by a cottonwood tree. Flora pulled a blue- checkered cloth from the hamper and spread it out, smacking Rufus' hand as he tried to reach for a snack.

It didn't take long for the foursome to demolish Annie's generous ham sandwiches, deviled eggs, and chocolate cake. Rufus pulled a yellow paper sack from his pocket and proudly held out four cookies.

"What are those? I've never seen a black and white cookie," Julia said.

"O-R-E-O. Look, it's stamped right on the top. What does that mean, Rufus?" Caleb asked and then bit into one of the dark biscuits. "Oh, they're stiff."

They ate the cookies, shaking their heads at this new product which they weren't sure would last. Rufus was crestfallen at the poor reception his treat had gotten. Then they began describing the sunset which Flora would see this evening and the beauty of the moon rising slowly out of the Gulf. "The train won't leave until nine o'clock. We'll dance at that pavilion over there," Caleb announced pointing to a white wooden open air building.

They wandered down to the boardwalk. Rufus and Caleb threw balls at the milk bottles but failed to knock enough down to win a prize, and the girls laughed uncharitably. A weight guessing game yielded them a velvet rabbit as all four were able to fool the hapless operator.

"Can you believe that sucker? One hundred forty-six pounds! What does he take me for? Some lightweight?" Caleb indignantly protested the man's guess.

"Well, he's never seen you put away food. No one would guess that those long arms and legs store so much groceries." Flora laughed.

The dark blue water dotted with white caps was inviting. Sharp cliffs rose from the small beach made of coarse dark sand. They walked out on the wooden pier, admired a large white sailing vessel that was passing by and wished for cane poles as silvery trout splashed around them in the surprisingly clear water. Next time they would bring their fishing gear.

Flora stood admiring the broad expanse of Galveston Bay then realized a group of picnickers was trying to get around her on the narrow pier. She moved over a little to let them pass and suddenly landed in the water, her feet dangling underneath her as she bobbed up and down looking for the bottom. Frantically, she waved as she saw her new straw hat floating out to sea. Giving it up as a lost cause, she began paddling toward the shore not realizing her motions had been interpreted by Rufus as a cry for help. He dove in the water and before she could protest, he was behind her, awkwardly thrusting his arms underneath hers.

"Rufus, let me go," Flora sputtered. She flailed her arms, trying to wrest herself from his viselike grip.

"I'm going to save you. Relax and you can float to shore." Rufus barked.

Flora looked at him and began laughing. He looked more comical than heroic. His red curls were plastered to his head,

124

and his blue bow tie listed to one side as the detachable starched collar spun around his Adam's apple. She tried to stop laughing for she could see the more she laughed, the madder Rufus was getting.

"Okay, just drown, darn you." Rufus released his hold on her and swam toward the bank, churning the water furiously with his angry strokes.

Flora followed behind him, and they both staggered up the embankment at the same time. The group on shore had gone from agitated concern to hysterical giggles as they watched the drama unfold. They clapped loudly when the water-sodden couple emerged from the bay.

"Why didn't you young folks bring a bathing costume if you wanted to swim?" The minister innocently pointed to the swimmers at the edge of the surf, women covered in black bloomers which came below the knees, black lisle stockings covering their legs. "I don't suppose either of you brought a change of clothes?" he asked hopefully.

"I didn't plan my swim, Sir." Flora looked dismally at her lovely white skirt and green and white jacket now covered with layers of sand. Her pompadour was destroyed, and her hair hung around her shoulders. She turned and looked balefully at the sea which had claimed her beautiful new bowler and announced, "I feel just as miserable as I look, Sir," Flora announced, her teeth chattering and her face a chalky white.

"Seems to me, you two need to go home. The train isn't due to leave for five more hours. Perhaps, Mr. Westcott will drive you in his automobile? He plans to leave soon."

The kindly member of Christ Church agreed to transport the pitiful twosome to town. Flora wrapped herself in the blue gingham tablecloth and a quilt, and the threesome clattered off down the narrow shell lane which connected with the main road between Galveston and Houston.

Flora soon realized Mr. Westcott was either a new automobile driver or suffered from very poor eyesight. He managed to hit every chughole in the road. When they finally connected with the main road, Flora looked at Rufus, relieved the bouncing was over, but he glared at her as if to say that this was her fault. She thought to herself, so much for my Sunday outing.

They reached downtown, and Flora offered to ride the trolley out to the Heights, but Mr. Westcott would not hear of it. She realized it was best that she not attempt to board a streetcar wearing a blue gingham tablecloth for a headpiece and a quilt for a shawl despite her eagerness to remove herself from her present company.

They drove down the Boulevard, and she directed the driver to her home. Rufus jumped out and silently held the door open. Flora thanked Mr. Westcott profusely and turned to her swimming companion. She tried not to grin as she watched his Adam's apple bobbing in his throat and his jaw muscles twitching angrily.

"It's been a picnic I'll never forget, Rufus. Thank you for coming to my rescue." She watched as he shook his head. "No, I mean it. It was sweet of you. I really appreciate it."

When he did not respond to her apology, Flora turned sadly and walked up the stairs, her head bowed, her arms tightly clutching the quilt. As she reached the front porch, she was dismayed by her unexpected visitor.

"What in the world have you done now, Miss Logan?" Max Andrews voice was incredulous.

Flora looked down at the Sunbonnet Sues which were marching down her limbs and across her front, and blinked back the tears. Cold, wet, and thoroughly dispirited, Flora was furious that Max Andrews should see her like this.

"You look like something the cat drug in." With that pronouncement, Max unfortunately chose to start laughing. While Flora had been only too willing to laugh at Rufus' sad appearance, she could find no humor in her own similar figure. Her haughty look cut Andrews guffaws short.

"Mr. Andrews, what an inappropriate time for you to have come calling. May I please excuse myself? I am somewhat indisposed." Flora stiffly extended her hand to him and caught her breath as he took it in his and brought it to his lips, kissing it lightly.

"I am afraid you just got a taste of Galveston Bay. Is it as salty now as it was when I took my swim?" Flora smiled ruefully.

"Let me see you inside, Miss Logan, and then I'll leave. I

am sorry I came. I only wanted to tell you how much I enjoyed our afternoon in the park yesterday."

She bid him good afternoon, and he spoke of telephoning her the next day. Grateful for his departure and for the peace and quiet of the house, she quickly went to the bathroom and drew a tubful of hot water, leaving a trail of soggy garments in her wake. Generously, she sprinkled the water with jasmine bath salts and climbed in, breathing a sigh of contentment.

After her bath she stretched out. As she drifted to sleep, she remembered she hadn't asked Max about his visit to see Mr. Fain. When she woke it was after dark and someone was loudly knocking on her bedroom door. Startled, she sprang up and flew to the door. "Annie, is that you?"

"Yessum, it's me. You got to get dressed and come quick. Something terrible's happened; it's awful, just awful."

Flora froze as every gruesome possibility flitted through her brain. She hurriedly dressed, put on her boots, lacing them only halfway in her haste to get to the door.

The first thing she saw when she entered the hallway were two officers wearing Houston Police Department badges. They stood stiffly with their hands behind their backs, staring at the rug.

"Yessir, what can I do for you?"

"You are Miss Logan, Caleb Logan's cousin? The one that has the marble yard?"

"Yes, I am. Why?"

"Miss Logan, we're Houston policemen asked by Constable Furlow to assist him. A man named Ward Fain has been found dead. We've been told he was your employee. Is that correct?"

"Dead." Flora's response was a statement rather than a question. To her, the officer's announcement was not a surprise. She'd known something else was going to happen. She'd never believed Caleb's reassurances that everything was going to be okay. Or Max Andrews' assumption that the private investigator could handle everything. "How?"

"Doc Robinson thinks it was poison, Miss." She watched the man shake his head in disbelief.

"What must I do?" Flora asked.

"We just wanted to notify you, Miss. He was found by a

Miss Rita Campbell. She said we should ask you what poison was used, that you know about these things. Is that correct?"

"What do you mean? I'm a botanist, and I am trained to know about plants and their uses, but I know little or nothing about how to use a plant to poison someone. Poisons are available at any pharmacy."

"Aha. But you do know a little. Right, Miss?"

Flora felt herself flushing with humiliation. "Gentlemen, I know nothing about Mr. Fain's death. If that's what you're suggesting, you have come to the wrong person." She clapped her hand on her mouth and wished for a hanky to help hide her fear. All she could hear were Max Andrews' words, "I'll take care of Ward Fain. I'll take care of Ward Fain." The deathly words resounded through her brain like a knell.

"Well, Doc Slataper'll know the cause after he examines the body. We'll have his results in a few days. We'll be talking to you, Miss Logan. Have a good evening, Miss." The officer turned as if to leave and looked back at Flora. "Where did you say you'd been this evening?"

CHAPTER THIRTEEN

After the police left, Flora sat at the kitchen table staring at the cup of steaming camomile tea Annie placed in front of her. She peered into the pale brown liquid, and knew she would need more than the properties of this herb to calm her pounding heart. Who killed Ward Fain? Rita had suggested her name to the police. "Why? Why did she accuse me? I didn't kill him, but who did? I must talk to Max."

Annie sat in the rocker, nodding her head; not speaking, but humming softly as the chair's wooden runners drummed the linoleum floor. "That's a good idear, Miss Flora."

What if Max had had words with Fain? She knew he couldn't have killed him. I know he's not capable of murder. She was surprised how strongly she felt about that. She wondered if he would have the same reaction to her capability for murder. He called her "impulsive" and "headstrong;" couldn't those be characteristics of a murderer?

Flora finally went to bed, but nightmares of Ward Fain interrupted her sleep. How can he still haunt me? She could hear his whiny little voice asking her "Miss Logan, why don't you stay where you should? Why are you always poking around in places where you don't belong? Why do you think you're so smart?" Morning came, gray and damp, and she began to re-examine the surprising death of Ward Fain.

While she considered him one of the most odious men she had ever known, she had difficulty believing that anyone hated him enough to poison him. What motive could anyone have had? She supposed that she actually had more of a motive than any-one. Who, other than Max and Dessie, knew about his abandonment of her in the Big Thicket? Was that fact known by someone who was using the incident to frame her for murder? If she knew the answer to this question, would she know who killed him? Was he really poisoned? That didn't sound like Robert Wilson's style. He would have used a strong-arm tactic. Something more physical.

The telephone rang and Annie's voice called to her. Flora arose from her bed, put on the wrapper she had flung on the chair, and went to the hall where Annie waited with the receiver.

129

"Thank you, Annie." She sat down beside the telephone and noticed that Annie stood listening. Oh well, she knew the housekeeper was still out of kilter from the police visit the night before. So was she. "Good morning, this is Miss Logan."

"What is this Miss Logan nonsense? Didn't Annie tell you it was me?"

"No, oh I'm so glad to hear your voice, Dessie." Flora's relief was evident. Annie gave a loud sigh and shuffled back in the kitchen.

"Remember Wednesday is the bridal luncheon at Helen Milroy's. Did you decide on the lavender silk?" Dessie didn't wait for an answer before she continued. "I'm wearing a white organdy frock over my French blue pelisse. I wore the dress last week, but with the white over it, it looks like another outfit entirely. I doubt anyone will be able to tell it's the same frock."

"That's a splendid idea, Dessie. You must have read the same article I did in *Ladies' Home Journal.*"

"Oh, no, you mean you saw it too? Oh shoot, everyone will know what I'm about. My wardrobe just won't go far enough to make the rounds of all these parties. I thought I'd sewed enough outfits, but I underestimated how social this wedding has become."

Flora could tell Dessie was close to tears. "It's okay. You haven't long now. Just two more weeks and you'll be the newest bride in the Heights. Wear the gray crepe you were saving for your trousseau, and we'll go shopping for more material and make another dress for you to take on your honeymoon." Flora gulped and said, "I'm not much help at the sewing machine, but I can cut and baste."

"Flora, I can't believe you're saying this. You wouldn't be caught dead with pincushions and scissors." Dessie announced this as if it were written in stone. "If you're sure you wouldn't mind helping me, I've got an even better idea. Let's go downtown and get some fabric and make a new dress to wear to the luncheon. We've got three days."

"I do need to go downtown and see Max Andrews, but I don't know about making a dress that fast. What if it doesn't turn out? That's crowding us a little. Maybe your aunt could help us?"

"Sure, that's a great idea. We'll get it started and say we're stuck. You know she can't resist a problem. Carter calls it her missionary zeal."

"I'll meet you in front of the trolley stand in two hours. I have an errand I need to run first."

"Thanks, Flora." Dessie hung up wondering where Flora was going, but she hadn't asked because she was pretty sure she didn't want to know. She knew Flora had never forgiven Ward Fain for his failure to come back for her. How badly had she hated him? Dessie was afraid. She had waited for her friend to tell about Mr. Fain's death.

Mrs. Akins, who lived next door to the boarding house where Fain lodged, had called Dessie at eight o'clock this morning to tell her that there had been a murder on the Boulevard. Dessie wondered what would she think if she knew that this might be the second?

"Wasn't he working at Logan's Marble Yard? Your friend Flora Logan probably knew him, didn't she?" Mollie Akins paused, but as Dessie said nothing, she continued. "I stayed in my house when the police came with a hearse, but I couldn't help noticing Miss Campbell ran out the door following the officers to the street. It was nighttime, all peaceful until she came out. She was screaming something terrible. I never saw anyone so worked up. Her black hair was streaming down her back and her white wrapper was flying away from her bosom. It was disgraceful, I'm telling you what. I watched because she was indecent and those policemen just looked and looked at her. The women of the Heights need to know about this kind of behavior. There's something real common about her, don't you think?" Again, she stopped, and when no answer was forthcoming, she babbled on.

"Well, I haven't told you the worst. Standing there like she was, right in the middle of the esplanade, that woman screamed, 'she did it. She killed him!'"

"Miss Akins, for heaven's sake, whom was she accusing?"

"Well, that's why I called. I wanted to be the first to tell you because it's just the awfullest thing. She said your friend's name over and over. Just yelling 'Flora Logan' out for everyone to hear."

131

Dessie nearly dropped the telephone receiver. Then she caught hold of herself and spoke sternly, "Mollie Akins, I don't intend to listen to another word of this gossip. I know Flora Logan better than anyone, and I know that she hasn't killed anyone. That's an outrageous lie! Rita Campbell just made that up. She's crazy as a fly in a drum."

"Well, I don't know about that, but I'm afraid your friend is in for some more trouble. Haven't you noticed how it just seems to follow her around?" Mollie Akins finished with a high-pitched giggle and bid Dessie good day.

Dessie was relieved to get rid of the busybody, but she had called Flora immediately. When her friend did not refer to Ward Fain's death, Dessie was puzzled and concerned. Maybe, Flora didn't know he was dead. She dismissed this as farfetched. Nothing travels faster than bad news. Well, perhaps, she didn't want to discuss it with me because of the bridal luncheon. It would be like her to want to spare me unpleasantness.

Actually, Dessie was close to the truth. Flora was loathe to burden her friend with this new disaster. She knew Dessie realized how close she came to being Ward Fain's enemy, and she hoped her friend was giving her the benefit of the doubt. She wanted to know what the city pathologist would find, but in the meantime she had her own questions about Ward Fain's death. Her errands that morning had included another visit to Mr. Thurow and then to visit the owner of the Red Cross Pharmacy.

At eleven she and Dessie met and boarded the streetcar for downtown. In twenty minutes, they got off at Main and Preston. "Do you want to go to Mr. Andrews' office first?" Dessie asked.

"No, I will go there later by myself."

Dessie gave her a quizzical look. Flora offered no explanation. They headed for Barringer-Norton's, and Dessie led the way to the back of the store. They walked up the wide wooden stairway to the second floor where the better fabrics were displayed.

The glass-topped wooden counters were stacked with bolts

of fabrics, the green Flora had admired in the window, as well as a beautiful burgundy gabardine, and a black and white houndstooth check. All the fall materials were displayed. Inside the glass cases were rolls of soutache braid in black, navy and brown. Nottingham lace and ruching and exquisite Swiss embroidered edging were displayed side by side. Another case held nothing but buttons. Dessie and Flora examined each of the fabrics carefully. After much deliberation, Dessie selected a foulard messaline.

"You don't think this gold makes my skin look sallow? I've never, never worn yellow."

"Not at all, and it's much richer than yellow. It has a luminous look about it. I've never seen the silk woven into a twill like this." Flora spoke enthusiastically.

The sales girl quickly picked up the conversation. "Oh, Miss, it's a wonderful piece of cloth. Just look at yourself in this mirror. That's right, stretch it out all the way to the floor. We've never gotten messaline in a shade like this. This piece has the new wide border design that's such a favorite in New York. I know it won't last long."

That settled it for Dessie. She and Flora sat at the table where the newest edition of Mr. Butterick's book lay. They poured over the one piece dresses, waists and skirts and selected a pattern which was shown made up in a similar bordered fabric. It was an afternoon gown with three-quarter sleeves, a simple empire bodice which was joined to a skirt that hung straight but not too straight.

"Carter made me promise that I wouldn't wear any more of those hobble skirts. He says men hate them because of the way they cause women to walk. Like little Oriental girls!"

"Oh, he just hasn't seen enough of them to get used to the style. They're the rage in New York City." Flora couldn't help feeling proud of her exposure to the fashion capitol of the nation.

"This is perfect, Dessie. We can whip this up in two shakes of a lamb's tail."

Dessie couldn't help laughing at Flora's assurance spoken as she knew from a total lack of knowledge about dressmaking. But she appreciated her friend's enthusiasm. "I wish we had time to make you a new frock as well."

"No, no, this is your day and you are the honoree. You'll shine in your new dress."

The clerk measured off the five yards which the pattern called for. She figured the cost of the fabric, double checking her total. "I have to be careful. I sold some silk brocade last week for thirty-five cents a yard. All our silks are fifty cents a yard. The store manager really gave me a set down. I almost lost my job."

Dessie paid, and they left the store and walked outside, both gasping excitedly.

"Oh, Dessie, it's the circus parade. Look, it's going to pass right in front of us." Flora turned to her friend, her brown eyes alight with merriment. "Remember how we used to come downtown for this parade?"

"Right, we never went to the circus performance. The parade was the thing. You were going to be a trapeze artist like the 'world-renowned glittering Gilda.'"

"Yes, of course. I remember the year you got dreamy-eyed over the ringmaster. You said he looked like a moving picture star," Flora laughed.

"Oh, no, look; it's the same ringmaster. I can't believe he's still in the circus. Why did I think he was handsome? He doesn't hold a candle to my Carter."

"You better say that, or I'll tell. Here come the elephants. This is my favorite."

"They're repulsive, and they smell like something dead." Dessie sniffed the air and wrinkled her nose. "I can already tell they're coming. You didn't need to announce it."

"Dessie, look at their eyes. See this first one coming. His eyes, I mean, his eye. . . I guess you really can't see both at one time." Flora stopped for a moment. "His eye shows how he feels about being a captive, about being in a dusty street, about being away from his jungle where it's cool and there's not a brass band blaring in his ear."

"Stop, you're going to make me cry or laugh, I'm not sure which," Dessie giggled.

"In the jungle, he's a great lord. Here, he's nothing but a . . ." Flora clutched Dessie's arm and pointed upward toward the building across the street.

"What are you looking at? Those men standing on the awning? Who are they?"

She saw Robert Wilson, head and shoulders above the other men and standing next to him was his rough talking brown-suited pal. Why were they up there? Where was the investigator who was supposedly watching them? Each had a tankard of ale, and brown-suit was smoking a cigar. They looked like they hadn't a care in the world. Why weren't they at work? Were they celebrating Ward Fain's death? They looked amused about something, that was evident. Abruptly, Walters pulled a small red book out of his coat pocket and Flora gasped realizing it looked like her father's journal.

Mesmerized by the sight of these two whom she had not seen since the day Chandler Parker died, and furious at their brazenness, Flora looked up and down the street. Before she could think of a way of getting across in the midst of the parade, a blood-curdling scream filled the air, and then another. People began pointing upward to the awning where Wilson and his friend were standing, and Flora realized with horror the reason for the screams.

The wooden awning, crowded to capacity with men who had come out of the upstairs poolroom to watch the parade, was cracking apart. The paralyzed crowd watched as the iron pole supporting the structure buckled, and the corner of the awning came crashing down. The men who had been standing near the support were first to fall. A couple of men who were standing back toward the building must have felt the platform giving way, and they jumped the twenty feet to the street below. One man who lost his balance as the porch tipped lower and lower, shot down the rapidly increasing incline like a cannon ball.

The scene was terrifying as Flora and Dessie and the hapless spectators watched the balcony full of men falling to the right and left and sliding down the tilting surface. Suddenly, their attention was directed to the cries of the women and children standing under the awning and now in grave danger of being crushed to death by the collapsing structure above them.

It was pandemonium, and Flora lost sight of Wilson and his friend. She and Dessie stood helplessly with the street full of people. Even if they had wanted to help, no one could cross the street, for the circus parade never stopped. They watched as the elephants lumbered by adding their intermittent raucous shrieks to the screams of the victims which now filled the air. A stranger to Flora's right sank to the pavement.

"Dessie, do you have your smelling salts? This woman's fainted." Flora dropped her parasol and knelt on the sidewalk. She took out the hatpins and removed the woman's straw bowler. Then she loosened her collar button and began fanning her with the paper parcel she still clutched in her hand.

"Here, this'll bring her around." Dessie knelt beside the stranger and held the vial to her nostrils. She was rewarded with flickering eyelids. The lady looked confused as if struggling to remember where she was and why she was lying on the cement.

"You fainted Ma'am. My friend and I were standing beside you. May we help you to your feet?" Flora spoke with a calm which she certainly did not feel. All around her were signs of serious panic as children began slipping through the parade between the elephants and the wagons.

"There's dead people over there. Somebody do something! A dead man just landed on top of me." A tow-headed hatless kid was waving his arms and yelling his news to everyone who stood there. That was all it took.

The stampede began with the crowd running toward the corner, pushing and shoving to get through the already congested area. Flora could see two ambulance wagons trying to come down Fannin, but the parade continued to block the street. The driver of Westheimer's rescue cart halted his horses and impatiently waited for the street to clear. Finally two policemen appeared and stepped between an elephant and a bright red wagon with iron bars occupied by a mangy African lion. As they did so, the lion emitted an horrific roar. The officers jumped a foot off the ground and retreated to the sidewalk.

Flora took advantage of the momentary halting of the parade to leave Dessie and cross the street. She could hear her friend's frightened cries, but she had to see what had happened to Wilson and Walters. She was determined not to let the journal get away from her again. Was Wilson the dead man the young

136

boy had seen? She started across Preston Avenue, waving her hand to dismiss her friend's yells and wending her way between the elephants. She halted, electrified as she heard a man's voice calling her name.

"Flora Logan, what are you trying to do?" The voice was filled with anger.

Flora looked over at the sidewalk she was trying hard to reach, and her heart sank as she realized who had spoken so commandingly. Max Andrews stood at the pavement's edge, his tall hatless figure rising above the crowd.

She muttered "Hell's Bells", skirted around the last of the elephants and came up to him and said, "Mr. Andrews, I think you've lost your hat."

He glared at her in disbelief as he took her arm in his and held it tightly. "Let's get out of here. Come on."

"Oh, Max, help me find Robert Wilson. He and Walters were on the awning and they fell. I think Walters had just handed him Papa's journal. Where's your man that was watching them?"

"What?" Then as her words sank in, he grabbed her arm and said, "Let's go." They inched their way across the street but saw no signs of either man. Disappointed, Flora searched the faces of the crowd pushing and shoving around them. Her eyes went to the sidewalk where a man was writhing with pain.

Just to the right of him, she saw it. The small red book lay on the pavement in front of her. She couldn't believe it. She reached down to retrieve it, elbowed Max, and handed it to him, pointing to his coat pocket.

"Can we go now?" Max asked worriedly.

"I can't leave without Dessie. Can you go over and find her?"

"You mean she's with you? No, I'm not leaving you for an instant. We'll go back together."

Flora was angry that he'd spoiled her chances of locating Robert Wilson's body, but she was elated over finding the journal and knew that Max Andrews was their best hope of getting out of this melee. She gripped his arm, and they started back across to the opposite side. Dessie dissolved into tears when she saw them. Later she would say they had been tears of happiness, but for now the woebegone face showed no sign of cheer.

They proceeded down Fannin, away from the teeming street filled with horses, elephants, crying children, hysterical men and women, and gray-coated officers rushing around as they tried to resolve an impossible situation. Two men were being loaded into the first ambulance. One man's arm hung crookedly at his side, and his face was covered with blood.

Flora and Dessie looked aside and hurried along beside Max, backtracking over to Prairie and then towards Main. Once they reached Main Street, the Scanlan Building loomed in front of them, and Max steered them inside and up the stairs. He threw open the door to his office and barked at his secretary, "Miss Sullivan, go and get something for these ladies." The secretary looked at him in confusion.

He sat them down on the couch, went over and poured three glasses of water. Then he went to the telephone which was mounted on the wall and asked the operator to get him Preston 152.

"Jessie, this is Max. I'm here in my office, but I just left the most awful disaster I have ever witnessed. You've already heard about it? Okay, your foreman Robert Wilson was standing on the Opera House Bar's awning that crashed to the ground." He paused and listened. "Yeah, I wonder why he was there, too. Weren't you going to fire him today? Maybe he got wind of that. He's bound to have been injured, but no one knows where he's been taken. Miss Logan is here with me; she saw him fall, but she lost sight of him after that. What she did find is her father's journal. I'm putting it in my safe right now."

He stopped and listened, then nodded. "That's why I wanted to call you. I think he's dangerous, Jesse. Fain's death may have resulted because he crossed Wilson, and Fred Logan may also have been one of his victims. Let's hope your detective can find him. Flora, I mean Miss Logan, says she feels sure he must have broken his leg, so he won't be able to travel too fast. Have your man check at the infirmary, though it's my bet he went to a doctor's office to avoid being noticed."

After Max hung up, he turned to Flora and Dessie. "I hope you understood what I was saying to Mr. Jones. The agency he hired was already on the case. We were about ready to close in when this happened. I think Wilson knew he was about to be

138

caught which explains why he wasn't at work. We'll get him, don't worry, Flora, and thanks to you we'll be able to prosecute him with evidence from the journal." He saw her concern and misunderstood the reason. "We'll take care of it."

"Max, I must look at the journal before you put it away."

He seemed surprised, but removed it from his breast pocket. She took the diary and went to a chair in the corner of the office. Max and Dessie chatted idly while she sat there reading. Then she came over and quietly told him of the page that troubled her.

"Your secret will be safe, Flora," he assured her. He patted her arm and turned to Dessie. "Are you ladies ready to leave?"

Both women nodded and Dessie said, "We'd better get home and start sewing."

Max's confusion caused them both to laugh.

"We're giddy with relief, Mr. Andrews. I'm sure I've never been so frightened in my life," Dessie explained.

Flora agreed and stood, looking down in amazement to see that she still had her parcel and her umbrella and her handbag. Dessie rose as well, checking to make sure her precious gold messaline had not been damaged. The ladies waited while Max Andrews got another hat to replace the one he'd lost in the street, and bade Miss Sullivan goodbye.

Max avoided the scene of the accident as he drove them home. When the buggy pulled up to Dessie's home, he alighted and helped the ladies do the same. Standing on the curb, he looked at Flora and said, "You scared me to death. When I saw you in the street, surrounded by those galumphing animals, I couldn't think what would happen next. Will you promise me that you'll be careful?" He lowered his voice and leaned toward her ear, "If you see Wilson, you must not go after him. Call this number on the telephone," he pressed a card into her hand. "These are the men Jesse Jones has hired. No more heroics, please. My heart can't stand much more."

Flora promised she would follow his advice about Wilson, shook his hand, holding on for a moment longer, and then went with Dessie up the sidewalk. She turned and gave him a last look and a wave as he started driving away.

"What can't his heart stand?" Dessie asked.

"I'm not sure," Flora replied.

CHAPTER FOURTEEN

Flora sat at the kitchen table, sipping her coffee and reading the morning paper's headlines. Delectable odors wafted through the air, and she looked indifferently at her cereal bowl filled with shredded wheat floating in milk, the soggy biscuits breaking apart. Annie stood at the stove, cooking hotcakes on the black iron griddle she had placed over the front burner. A plate of nicely browned pork sausages sat on top of the warming shelf to her right above the oven.

"Annie, why do you make these breakfasts? You act like you're feeding farm hands. We're city folks; we don't eat lumberjack breakfasts." Flora spoke testily.

"Mister Caleb said he would be here to take a break about nine o'clock. He has to get up earlier now that Mr. Fain's crossed over that bar; he comes back when he's done starting the cutters to working and eats breakfast."

"I guess I'm gone by then. I've never had such an unrestful vacation in my life. I'll have to go back to New York City for my life to calm down."

"Well, after what you and Miss Dessie saw on Monday, I'm wondering how you can sleep at night. I never heard of such in all my born days."

"Listen to what the paper says, 'In less than five minutes after the wooden awning fell, a report was spreading from mouth to mouth through the vast throngs that filled the downtown streets, that five or more people had been killed, and many more seriously, if not fatally injured.'" Flora stopped and took another sip of her coffee. "It happened just that fast, Annie. Dessie and I stood there and watched open-mouthed. The paper doesn't list any fatalities though it talks about the injured. I wonder if anyone was killed?" Flora especially wondered what had happened to Robert Wilson.

"Miss Flora, is that the doorbell?" Annie asked turning to

listen. She held up a widespread hand and motioned Flora toward the front door. "Could you answer that bell? I'm knee-deep in frying these cakes."

Flora laughed at Annie's culinary dilemma, rose and went to the hall. She stopped dead still as she saw uniformed officers standing at the door. The doorbell rang again, harshly insistent. She hastened to the entrance, her feet moving with more enthusiasm than she felt.

"Yes, Gentlemen, what can I do for you?"

"Well, Miss Logan, we're sorry to trouble you again, but we got Doc Slataper's report on the death of Mr. Ward Fain and we'd like to ask a few questions, if that's okay?"

"Certainly, come in." She led them into the living room and motioned them to take a seat on the banquette. They each removed their dark gray helmets. Flora remained standing.

The officer who had spoken to her at the door began. He seemed to be in charge and introduced himself as Sergeant Ryan. A barrel-chested, burly fellow, he had dark, curly hair damp with perspiration or hair oil, she couldn't tell which. His complexion looked like cream-colored candle wax accented by bright pink cheeks. Dark mutton-chop whiskers covered the lower part of his face, and he was chewing tobacco or something.

"Miss Logan, there's no sense in beating about any bushes. Doc Slataper says the deceased man was poisoned, and judging from the contents of his stomach, the poison was something he ate rather than drank. What I mean to say is that he ate poisoned food, and what do you suppose that would have been?"

"How would I know what Ward Fain ate for his last supper?"

"Miss Logan, Mr. Fain's companion, Miss Rita Campbell said the meal he ate was prepared in your kitchen, in this very house."

"What? She's mistaken. He wasn't here for dinner."

"We know that. We've checked you out pretty good, Miss. But this ladyfriend of his says your cousin Caleb came over Saturday with a plate of food. He told Fain he was going to a picnic Sunday and wouldn't be home for dinner. He claimed your cook had prepared extra food and now it was going to go to waste if he didn't give it away."

141

Flora opened and closed her eyes slowly and concentrated on not showing any reaction to what he'd just said. Her first thought was relief that the police weren't accusing Max Andrews of preparing some poisonous concoction. Then she realized whom Officer Ryan had implicated and gasped. "That sounds like something Caleb would do."

Officer Ryan heard her muttered reply. "Prepare a poisonous dish? Oh what a family!" He laughed mirthlessly and then continued. "Anyway, Miss Campbell says that's the last thing Fain ate on Sunday, and a couple of hours later, he started complaining about a scratchy throat and prickling lips. She left and went to Red Cross Pharmacy to get some medicine. When she returned his face was flushed with fever, and he fell on the floor when he tried to get out of bed, complaining that he was dizzy." The officer paused for emphasis as if enjoying the dramatic effect of his tale. "Through the early evening, he became worse. He began sweating through his shirtsleeves and had to take off his collar and cuffs because he was so hot."

"Did she speak of his having a headache?" Flora asked.

"Yes, she did; how'd you know?" the officer responded.

Flora urged him to finish his story. When he spoke of Fain's convulsions and shortness of breath, she felt chilled to the bone. A suffocating fear descended upon her and she sank into the nearby chair.

"Are you okay, Miss?" The officer asked, not unkindly.

"Yes, I'm fine. Please continue."

"Well, Miss, he died at 8:30 P.M. Sunday evening, and like I told you before, Doc says it was poison which killed him. He don't know for sure what it was, but he thinks from the way his insides looked, it was probably belladonna. Do you know anything about belladonna, Miss Logan?"

Flora knew a lot about this plant. Anyone who had ever studied botany knew about the Nightshade family, the plant which is said to be tended by the Devil himself. Despite its deadliness, the name belladonna, meaning "fair lady", is what the plant had always been called, supposedly because in early days Italian women dropped the juice from the berries into their eyes to enlarge the pupils and make the eyes more beautiful. She had been trained like all botanists to recognize the leafy, smooth

142

branched stem, the dull green alternate leaves of unequal size, and the single bell-shaped purple flowers. She could still see the drawing from Gray's *Field Manual of Botany*, but what else was she seeing? Flora shook her head, and sadly answered the officer, "Yes, I probably know more about belladonna than most people here in the Heights. All except one."

"Who's that, Miss?"

"The person who poisoned Ward Fain, Sir." He ignored her reply.

"Tell me, Miss Logan, did you or any member of your family have a reason to wish Mr. Ward Fain dead? Did you instruct your housekeeper to put belladonna or any foreign substance into the dish which she prepared on Saturday, supposedly for the family members?"

"Would you like to ask her?" The officer nodded, and Flora called out to Annie. They waited as the housekeeper shuffled in from the kitchen.

"Yes, Miss Flora, what you need now?" she asked sullenly. Obviously, she had peeked and knew who their company was.

"Annie, these officers would like to ask you about the cooking you did Saturday. What dishes did you prepare that Caleb might have taken over to Ward Fain?"

"I'm right sure it must've been that calves' liver and onions I fixed. The livers and the glass dish they was in waddn't here when I came in Sunday night, and they never showed up since."

"Ah, ha. Did you make a nice cream gravy to go over the liver?" the officer asked cunningly.

"Why, whoever heard of it being fixed any other way? Annie asked indignantly.

"Don't get smarty with me. This is a murder case and don't either of you forget it." The officer ran his short pudgy fingers through the greasy curls on his forehead while he paused to think.

"Let's see if I got this right? I've got a young lady who admits that she knows all about the poisonous plant belladonna, and I've got a cook who, probably taking directions from the aforementioned lady, cooked up some liver and onions for the deceased Mr. Fain. Neither of you would care to explain these circumstances, I don't suppose?"

"Officer, before we go any further, I should call my attorney. Your suggestions seem rather derogatory of my household. I'll just ring him up." Flora started for the telephone instrument.

"No, no, Miss. That won't be necessary. I'm just thinking out loud. No harm meant. Let's go, Officer Smith." He turned toward the front door, then remembered his manners and wheeled his chubby body around and gave Flora a bouncing bow. "Don't be planning any trips, please, Miss Logan."

Flora closed and locked the door behind the officer and collapsed on the hall chair. She looked at Annie in amazement. "What next? My head is spinning. I'm getting afraid to leave my bed in the morning."

"Well, right this minute, you has to get dressed, and walk outside pretty quick now if you gonna be at Miss Milroy's wedding thing for Miss Dessie. You need me to press that ribbon for your sash?"

"Glory be, I nearly forgot the party. What time is it?" She bounded into the living room where the clock rested on the fireplace mantel. "Thank goodness, I still have over an hour. Turn on the Hotpoint."

"Miss Flora, why doesn't you call Mr. Andrews right now? I'd feel better knowing he was watching over things happening with those policemen. We don't want them coming after us anymore. I hear they lock people up and throw away the key."

"Oh, I was just bluffing. I would never have called Max Andrews to come and rescue me. I'm not worried about their suspicions." Flora's bravado resounded through the room. "Pretty soon, the police will be handed the private investigator's report from Mr. Jones, and they'll know about Robert Wilson's disappearance. When they do, they will put two and two together and hopefully come up with four."

Annie stood frowning. "You may has convinced youself of that, but you ain't convinced me."

She went to dress and was amazed that she was able to find her clothes. Her arms moved mechanically, and she tasted the metallic flavor of fear, a new experience for Flora. Who had poisoned Ward Fain? The only motive she and Max had come up with was a deal with Robert Wilson that went sour. She doubted Wilson would have coldly planned a poisoning, a death that by design implicated Caleb and her as the murderers. She wanted to scream when the policeman told about Caleb taking over the dish of food. The idea of her cousin's planning a murder was ludicrous, planning ahead was not Caleb's forte. But someone had to have been capable of a carefully executed crime. The botanical drawing of the belladonna plant kept coming to her mind. What was she failing to see?

"A luncheon was given on October twenty-fifth by Helen Milroy for Bride-to-be Dessie Trichelle at 1107 Boulevard. The twenty-six guests were greeted in the foyer by Miss Milroy, who was a vision of loveliness in a powder blue silk surrah, the Bride-to-be Miss Trichelle, wearing a fashionable gown of gold messaline, and her attendant, Miss Flora Logan. Miss Trichelle was presented with a Tussie Mussie made of flowers and herbs the hostess gathered from her beautiful gardens. The odiferous nosegay contained rosemary, thyme, southernwood artemisia and lambs ears all of which surrounded one perfect pink rose. The greenery was edged with a lace ruffle, and the stem of the bouquet placed in a sterling silver holder which was Miss Milroy's gift to the bride. Tall silver urns filled with bronze chrysanthemums, purple asters, burgundy amaranth, and white gladioli adorned the front parlor of Judge Milroy's home, one of the most elegant on the Boulevard.

The luncheon tables were covered with pink damask cloths, and Miss Milroy used her mother's Haviland "Apple Blossom" china to serve a delicious meal of eight covers and four courses. Adorable saltine cracker baskets, filled with chunks of pineapple and white grapes, were tied together with narrow pink satin ribbon and placed to the right of each place setting. Among the many delectable dishes were Miss Milroy's famed chicken croquettes. For dessert the guests had their choice of Sultana raisin tarts, prune whip or snow pudding. It was

*an elegant event. Miss Trichelle will marry Carter
Stanley on November 10th."*

- *The Suburbanite*, October 27, 1912.

It was the most awful party Flora had ever attended. The
nightmare began with the first guest's arrival and continued
until the last guest departed. Flora supposed in any small town,
news traveled at the same lightning speed which it did in Houston Heights. Everyone there knew about Ward Fain's death on
the Boulevard. The poisoning was the newest topic of conversation, yet because everyone knew the police had come twice to
question Flora Logan, not one of the ladies intended to bring up
a subject which might be too painful for her. Their politeness
could only extend so far, however, and Flora was quizzed dis-
creetly by each one of them.

Mrs. Jenkins, her next-door-neighbor, asked her if her
trip back to New York had been delayed. Jane Nelson wanted to
know if she thought she would ever live in the Heights again.
Nellie Swanson wondered why she hadn't stayed for the evening's
dancing at Sylvan Beach. Janie Jordan asked her slyly if she
had been down to see the Rice Hotel job site where her cousin
was working. One dowager tightly corseted into a hideous satin
heliotrope gown, leaned over and whispered, "How do you like
the police department's new gray uniforms?"

By the time lunch was finished and the ladies had adjourned to the sun porch, Flora made a beeline for a wicker
chair in the far corner. She unconsciously picked at the flowered chintz cushion, pleating and unpleating the ruffle as the
afternoon wore on, planning her course of action. Finally when
she thought she could not stand another moment, the guests
rose and took their leave, and Flora, as hastily as etiquette per-
mitted, followed suit.

She walked toward her home, but instead of turning on
Ninth Street, she crossed the Boulevard and went to the trolley
stop. The streetcar was coming, and she jumped aboard and
deposited her nickel. She rode to Main Street and McKinney,
got off and walked over to Travis where she bounded up the

146

broad curved stairs of the Carnegie Library. The room with its white-washed plaster walls and dark pine woodwork, where she had spent so many hours during her senior year at Heights High, barely grazed her consciousness as she went to the main desk, intent on her mission. The librarian stared at her, and Flora blushed realizing how odd she must look, standing there in her lavender silk afternoon gown; inappropriate research attire. Ignoring her questioning stare, she asked for directions and proceeded to the section which she sought. Once there she meticulously examined each of the books. When poisoning was suggested by the police, she had gone to Red Cross Pharmacy to talk with Mr. Sureau. According to the pharmacist, several poisons were available although some had to be signed for. She was reassured momentarily because druggists' lists would be easily traceable by the police, but when the police report stated the poison was belladonna, she had gone to see Mr. Thurow.

He confirmed that the plant was not carried by any nursery and would have to be imported by someone who had knowledge of poisonous plants. He was the one who suggested that she come here where the information she sought might be available. She did not have high hopes, certain this would be far too simple a way to uncover a murderer, but she was so desperate she dared not give it a try.

Her scrutiny included only this section of books, and bystanders observing her actions would have found them odd indeed. She pulled each card from the envelope on the inside cover and examined the names of those who had checked out the book. Shaking her head in doubt, she almost missed what she sought. She reread the cramped signature and gasped as she realized this had to be the answer, strange as it seemed. Her cry earned her a stern frown from the librarian; ignoring the woman's disapproval, Flora went to the desk. She asked to borrow a pencil and paper and returned to the book where she had found the name of the suspected murderer. She copied the title, author, and dates the book was checked out over the last month, and checked entries in the index, turning to the pages indicated and skimming the information given. When she finished, she went back to the librarian, handed her the pencil and asked to check out the book. Her old library card had expired, and she spent several minutes filling out an application and convincing the woman to waive the waiting period and let her have the book to take with her. She was sure the librarian questioned her sanity, but fortunately decided to go along with her request.

After she left the library, Flora walked back to Main Street, but before she caught the trolley for home, she entered a small two story building shaded by a bright yellow canvas awning on which was printed in large black letters "Art Jackson's Photography Studio." Dessie had told her about this shop and said the owner would be coming out to the Heights to take their wedding photographs. Flora immediately spotted what she was looking for. She picked up a small box camera, pleased that it was so lightweight. "It couldn't weigh over two pounds," she exclaimed.

"Miss, it weighs only one and a half; it's a perfect camera to take on a trip. Are you leaving soon?" The young clerk spoke eagerly. Flora ignored the question.

The price printed on a card stated $2.75. "Is this the correct price?"

"Yes, Miss, it is. This is the last of our stock. We'll be getting a newer, better model next week, if you'd like to wait. It'll be about the same price." His sales pitch fell on deaf ears.

Flora was relieved because she expected to pay more. She watched impatiently while the salesman instructed how to use the camera and loaded the daylight roll film, which made six exposures without having to be reloaded. He assured her it was a good camera for beginners, no focusing was needed and even a child could operate it. Satisfied this would meet her needs, she paid for the merchandise, and the gentleman provided a sturdy cloth satchel for her to carry it in. As she was leaving he called out to her to bring back the box with the roll film still in it, and he would take care of unloading it and having the prints developed.

A determined Flora Logan returned to Houston Heights on the five o'clock streetcar, making one more stop before she went home. Exiting the trolley at Center Street, Flora crossed the esplanade and approached Logan's Marble Works. She stood for a few minutes studying the front of the simple white frame building. Then she went to the edge of the sidewalk. Carefully, she took out her new camera and aimed it at the front of the building. She snapped all six shots and then left.

When she returned home, she called to Annie who came out of the kitchen wiping her hands on her apron, announcing that supper would be ready in an hour. In the privacy of her bedroom, Flora changed clothes, sat down on her bed, and studied the information she had gathered. She took the camera, wrapped it in a piece of flannel sheeting and hid it at the bottom of her wicker clothes hamper along with the library book. Her chest felt tight and her hands shook, for the information she concealed would probably be used to convict a person of murder.

All the pieces had slipped into place this afternoon, leaving only one remaining gap, and that was the why? What motive was strong enough to cause someone to kill two people, for Flora was convinced that the murderer had killed Fred Logan as well as Ward Fain. Love of money, greed, ambition, or was it something else entirely? The reason eluded her, but she knew that it was up to her to confront the murderer with her knowledge, and she knew she must do it as soon as possible. Briefly, she considered the idea of alerting the police, but felt that action would cause a dangerous delay. Unless she missed her guess, the guilty party was getting ready to leave town. She was startled to hear Annie calling her to dinner. Reluctantly, she put aside her thoughts of tomorrow, determined to say nothing about her plans to anyone. She turned out the electric light hanging down in the center of the room and calmly closed her door, reassured by the knowledge that she had positive proof after months of doubt.

As she walked into the front hall, she could smell chicken frying, and saw that the dining room table had been set for an extra person. She was surprised something special had been planned without her knowledge. She looked at the table, shaking her head, and thinking ruefully that this must be another of Annie's efforts to bring a sense of normalcy to their home. She wasn't exactly in the mood for company after the luncheon today, and she walked into the kitchen astounded by what she saw.

"Mr. Andrews, I'm sorry, I didn't know you had stopped

149

by. Annie, why didn't you call me?"

"I invited him, Miss Logan. I thought he could come over and eat supper and then maybe you and him could have a little talk."

Flora could feel blood rushing to her face. At that moment she wanted to throttle the busybody housekeeper. "Excuse me, Mr. Andrews, I'm afraid that much as I love Annie, this time she has gone too far. I'm happy that you'll be here to share our evening meal, though. I should've thought to invite you before now."

Annie added, "You shore should've, Miss Flora. What's a poor bachelor gonna eat every night? That boarding house food gets old fast. Anytime you got to cook for thirty people as cheap as you can, you gonna have boring food, I can tell you that."

Flora and Max laughed, and Max nodded his head in agreement. "I cook occasionally in my apartment kitchen, but the Rossonian is so modern, the feeling of the place is rather antiseptic. Regardless of how fully equipped it might be with all the modern conveniences, an apartment building is just not a home. It's an elegant place to hang my hat, but not very welcoming. I guess that's why I tend to take most of my meals at the boarding house. I'd rather eat with a bunch of people I don't know than eat alone. I hate eating alone."

Flora smiled in sympathy and realized that much of what he had said echoed her thoughts about Aunt Ruth's apartment building in New York. She loved the convenience of a well-planned floor design, but she hated not being able to look out the windows and see anything but more buildings. Since she had been home, she also realized how much she enjoyed having her own yard. The Botanical Gardens were grand and glorious, but you missed the pride of ownership, the sense of accomplishment that she felt when she and her mother had laid out the garden and tended it so carefully. Her dreamy thoughts were interrupted by Max and Annie.

"Yes, I absolutely agree with you, Annie. I think fried chicken shouldn't be restricted to Sunday lunch." Max complimented the cook on having thoroughly whetted his appetite.

She beamed with pride and pointed to the black skillets

filled with plump pieces of chicken browning in the Crisco. "When I ordered these chickens, I told that man I don't want you to send me any of those aeroplane chickens."

"What do you mean?" Flora asked.

"Those ones that's all wings and machinery and no meat."

They were laughing as the back door banged open, and Caleb entered, drawing back in surprise when he saw Andrews. "Hey, you're the fellow that's Mr. Jones' friend, aren't you?"

"Yes, I'm Max Andrews and you must be Caleb Logan, Miss Logan's cousin."

"Hey, Annie, if this is what it takes for you to make apple pies, we should have lawyers as company every night." Caleb walked over to the counter where two pies sat cooling, then he sidled up to the stove where Annie stood stirring flour into the leftover oil. "What's he doing here?" he whispered to the cook. She shook her head and put her finger to her lips.

Fortunately, Max and Flora had launched into a noisy discussion about the liability of the Opera House Bar owner who allowed the men to stand on the awning and thereby caused its collapse. Flora quoted from the paper which had stated that the poolroom manager had repeatedly warned patrons not to stand outside on the awning.

"Yes, but as long as they are on his property, he is liable for the damages," Max pointed out.

"Hey, why don't we all go to the Majestic tonight? There's a Ragtime Trio playing that's supposed to be great." Caleb loudly addressed the couple, ignoring their conversation.

"Oh, I don't know, Caleb. I have had a pretty full day."

"Come on, Flo, please. You haven't done a thing since you got here except fret and worry and run around getting into trouble." He watched as she indignantly raised her shoulders and put her hands on her hips. "Now, now, no use getting your dander up."

Flora started to protest and then looked over to see Max smiling wickedly. She grinned at him and rolled her eyes. "Okay, you win. What time's the show?"

Annie smiled at Flora approvingly, then folded her arms across her chest and beat out an imaginary rhythm with her long handled wooden spoon. She surprised the group by breaking out into the refrain, "Everybody's doin' it, doin' it. . ."

"Where did you learn ragtime?" Caleb asked laughingly.

"Mister Caleb, don't you be selling me short, I knows about most everything what's important. And ragtime is just that. It's Black folks' music, that's what."

"I haven't seen a vaudeville show since I left here four years ago. Now are you happy?" Flora smiled good-naturedly at Annie and Caleb.

Annie looked over at Flora and Max standing together. She winked broadly and said,"Yessirree, I am that."

Annie's solo broke the ice, and the threesome proceeded to sit down in the dining room and do justice to the wonderful meal she had prepared for them. Groaning, Max and Caleb helped Flora carry the dishes into the kitchen where they all three declined the deep dish apple pie with cheese which Annie expected them to eat.

"We'll wait until we come back. I shouldn't have had that second helping of cream gravy," Caleb moaned miserably.

Annie tried to act miffed, but chuckled to herself as if in triumph. "That's fine with me. Don't you be forgetting it's here waiting. Be sure to stay long enough to do justice to my sweets, Mr. Andrews."

"Oh, Annie, who could forget to eat your apple pie?" Flora smiled in appreciation.

Max quickly added, "Personally, I have always subscribed to Eugene Field's poem about the subject content of his prayers."

When I undress me/Each night, upon my knees/
Will ask the Lord to bless me/With apple pie and cheese.

They all howled with laughter at the thought of the hefty-sized Andrews on his knees praying nightly for food.

"Mr. Andrews, you should try Flora's cooking some time. Her pies are pretty near as good as mine." Annie looked incredibly innocent as she said this, and when Flora and Caleb burst into laughter at the audacious lie, she simply cleared her throat and began singing again, this time accompanying herself with a soft-shoe dance. The laughter was no more than one would have expected at the sight of the short, plump woman, her grey hair

152

knotted tightly at the back of her head, wearing a large white apron, waving her spoon and wiggling her bottom all over the kitchen.

The group continued laughing as they walked to the trolley stop, and no one remembered to question Flora's culinary abilities again. Since Annie's motive had been rather obvious, Flora looked up several times at Max Andrews, wondering if he had been embarrassed by the housekeeper's amateur attempts to manipulate them.

But Max Andrews acted as if he were having the time of his life. He and Caleb reminisced about baseball games they'd seen and the upcoming Texas A&M and University of Texas football game, the sports highlight of the fall. She admired his easy ways, the fact that he seemed to charm everyone from Annie to Caleb, from Hortense Ward to Annette Finnigan. She wondered what his secret was and finally decided that he must like himself. He likes who he is, and she remembered Thurow had said a man is valued according to his own estimate of himself. She fell to considering whether or not she liked who she was. Recognizing the impetuosity and volatility which formed much of her personality, she wondered if maybe she could change these things about herself. She decided that a tempering would be possible if she had a person in her life who accepted her with all her shortcomings and who could tease her about them instead of constantly finding fault as her father had done. She scolded herself for idly daydreaming about the future knowing, as she did, what waited for her the following day and the serious consequences which could result.

"You're quiet tonight, Miss Logan," Max Andrews' deep voice interrupted her thoughts.

Flora smiled, not offended by his prying but pleased by his attention. She was grateful that the trolley's clicking wheels rolled to a stop, and she was spared from responding to his comment. The three got off and walked over to Congress where they purchased tickets at the box office and entered the theater.

Max Andrews noticed several times that evening the wicked mischievous look in Flora's dark brown eyes, and he should have been forewarned that she was up to something. But, unfortunately, he did not know the extent of her daring.

He had been dissatisfied with the agency's report on Robert Wilson. The foreman had vanished and while the ticket agent at Grand Central thought he might have sold him a one-way ticket to St. Louis, they had no real proof. To Andrews, Wilson had masterminded the entire scheme which had resulted in both murders. Fred Logan was killed when he threatened to expose Wilson's actions to Jesse. Ward Fain had probably been eliminated for wanting a larger percentage of the payoffs. When Max turned over the reports he received to the Houston police, he was relieved that Flora was content to let the professionals take over. She could not continue to place herself in jeopardy and remain unscathed.

CHAPTER FIFTEEN

Pounding rain and rumbling thunder woke Flora the next morning. It was late for a hurricane, but early for a norther. Either way it wasn't going to stop her. She quickly penned a note, dressed and grabbed her umbrella from the stand, slipping out the front door before Annie could realize that she had arisen. She didn't want to lie to her or argue with her; leaving quietly seemed the simplest way.

As she got on the streetcar, she sighed in relief at the familiar conductor. Sam Danna looked at her in surprise when he heard her request but assured her he would see that the envelope was delivered. He waved aside the money she held out to him. Flora sank to the wooden bench and stared at the rain-filled boulevard.

As the trolley braked in front of Logan's Marble Works, she saw the flower beds and the holes, now filled with water, where the belladonna had been. That was all the vindication she needed. Any doubts she had were now dispelled.

She stood under the metal awning and shut her umbrella, leaning it against the planter box. Rain fell all around her, and she shivered with excitement. Twisting the knob, she was surprised to find the front door locked. She checked her watch, reached up and sharply rapped on the door. She could hear rapid footsteps from inside. Finally, the bolt was drawn, the door cracked open, and Flora looked into the eyes of the murderer.

Her stomach knotted and her hands fisted tightly. She wet her lips with her tongue and pushed her bottom lip under her upper teeth to calm the pounding in her chest. Someone once told her there is a courage which grows out of fear. Right now, the idea seemed idiotic.

"Whatcha want, Lovey? Caleb's not here."

"Rita, may I come in? I told my attorney I would get papers he needed to probate my father's will. He's at the courthouse waiting for me to bring them," Flora lied glibly.

"Sure, come on in."

She pushed open the door and slammed it shut as hard as she could. Startled, Rita fell back into the room. Flora noted the

155

open drawers and heavy leather satchel on the floor. "Where're you going?" She received no answer. "Are you packing the papers I need? That's kind of you." Flora sneered at Rita, surprised the woman wore a striped house dress istead of a traveling costume.

"It's none of your business, honey. Let's just say I'm moving up in the world and leaving this one-horse town behind."

"You're a tough nut, Rita. Seems to me you've diminished the population of this one-horse town by two."

"What in hell are you talking about?"

Flora ignored the question. "Are you taking your belladonna plants with you?"

"Am I taking what?"

"The belladonna you planted as part of your 'flower' beds in front of the office, the belladonna you used to poison Ward Fain."

"Aw, you're crazy; everybody in the Heights knows it. Ward used to say, 'she's crazy and mean,'" Rita giggled hideously. One time he told me, 'Rita, that Flora Logan's mean as a snake.'"

"How strange because as mean as I might be, I wasn't mean enough to kill him. You did that yourself, Rita, and I have the evidence to prove it."

"You have nothing."

"I have a photograph which I took yesterday of the belladonna you've been growing in front of this building until you dug it up this morning, a plant with no legitimate garden or landscape uses."

"That doesn't prove anything. I know nothing about plants. If anything like that's been growing there, you planted it. You're the plant lady, and everybody knows it."

"Oh, well, if asked, I could tell 'everybody' that your name is on the checkout list of all books on poisonous plants in the Carnegie Library downtown."

Rita's mouth dropped open and for the first time since Flora arrived, she looked uneasy. Flora plunged doggedly ahead. "Were you in love with Ward Fain?"

Rita laughed scornfully. "He was the dumbest 'fraidycat I ever knew. I was always smarter than that one. Afraid of his own shadow, he was. Always made me do his dirty work."

"What dirty work did you do for Mr. Fain? Kill my father?"

Flora took a stab in the dark and from the startled look on Rita's face, saw she had struck a blow but was shocked by the response.

"Fred?" Rita drew her shoulders up and lifted her head proudly. "I loved Fred Logan. He was old enough to be my pa, but I loved him. I thought he loved me too. I thought we were gonna be married."

"He threw you over, Rita, didn't he?" Flora asked softly.

The woman standing in front of her crumpled. Her face twisted like a corkscrew, and she squeezed each side of her head as if to press away a bad memory.

"I can still hear his words. He said I wasn't proper enough for him. He came in that evening and pulled out his checkbook." Rita stopped and wiped her eyes on her sleeve. "He said he didn't know what came over him, but that he couldn't be with me any longer. I wasn't the right kind of woman. That I would have to leave the marble works. He gave me the air like I was just an employee he had to let go. I made him a cup of tea, and after that the rest was easy." Flora watched her crying wondering whom her tears were for.

"God's sake, get ahold on yourself, Dearie." The unforgettable whine of Widow Parker's voice came from the doorway leading to the inner office. Stunned, Flora whirled around, grimacing when she saw that her ears had not deceived her.

"Don't Dearie me. You're in this just as deep. Don't think I won't tell that you fixed Ward's last dinner."

"We're not into nothing. I've packed and now we'll catch the train. Soon as we find Bobby, we'll be in tall cotton." The widow stood like a load of bricks daring Flora to open her mouth.

"I thought you were too lazy to get out of your own way, Mrs. Parker," Flora unwisely quipped.

"This 'uns too smart by half, Rita. We got to shut her up."

"No, Bertie, no more killings. I ain't using that belladonna again."

"You drugged my father with the belladonna, didn't you? Who pushed him under the trolley?" Flora demanded.

"Not me, I was still in Alabama," Widow Parker barked.

Rita's eyes hardened, and she glared at Bertie, then Flora. "Get out, Miss; get out while you can."

"Fain always appreciated you? He valued your work? He knew you were smarter than anyone else?" Flora turned each statement into a question to stoke Rita's anger. "Or did he consider you a liability? Did he think you couldn't be trusted? Did he tell you to leave like my father had?"

Flora flinched at the look on Rita's face and suddenly knew how foolish she had been to come here alone. But she could only lose by backing down now. She matched Rita's glare, holding her own as she tried to remember who had said, "Hell hath no fury like a woman scorned." Regardless of who wrote the words, she finally had a motive for the murders. What would Rita do next?

"We gotta lock her up and get outta here."

Flora saw what was coming, but before she could get her legs in motion, the two women pushed her toward the cloak closet. She screamed, but a weak cry was all that came out.

"My, my, Miss Logan, you society ladies yell softer than regular folks. That's good luck for us, not that there's anybody to hear you." Both women laughed heartlessly. "Saturday's crew is working at the hotel, so believe me when I say the yard is empty."

Bertha Parker opened the closet and pushed her in. The door slammed in Flora's face, and for a few moments she could hear nothing but a ringing in her ears. Then Rita shouted, "Stand there in the dark and practice on it, Miss Fancy Britches. Maybe you can come up with a real woman's yell that can be heard by someone outside this room." Flora could hear their laughter diminishing as they left the room.

Her head was pounding so hard she could hardly think. Palms outstreched, she braced herself against the door and breathed deeply. She had to calm down and make a plan if she were to prevent the departure of the two women. Once they were out of town, the chances of apprehending them would be slim. She put her ear to the door and listened, but all was quiet. Surely, they haven't left. As she stood there in the inky blackness of the closet, Flora smelled the eau de Cologne Rita favored. Something jasmine, she thought. Curious as to what the woman was leaving in this closet, she reached up and lifted the garment hanging on the coathook behind her. It felt like a man's coat. She reached up higher and lifted down a man's broad-brimmed hat. Both smelled of Rita's perfume. She was puzzled, but then remembered Mr. Thurow's description of the man he had seen running toward the railroad tracks the night her father was killed. A short person wearing a long sloppy coat and a hat with a big brim. Peculiar clothing for a warm August evening. Of course, that was it. The "man" had been Rita Campbell. She drugged his tea with the belladonna, just enough to incapacitate him then followed him as he walked to the trolley stop. A slight push would have sent him to his death under the streetcar's wheels. She realized if this were so, Rita's actions were premeditated, and Fred Logan's murder was not a crime of passion committed by a spurned woman.

What was Widow Parker's role? She hadn't been here for the first murder; why had she helped Rita murder Fain? It had to be about money. Even though Rita had teared up when she talked about Fred Logan, Flora felt her real sorrow had been the lost opportunity for his money. She must have killed Fain for money as well. Maybe he was going to cut her out, but what money were they splitting? It had to be money coming from the Rice Hotel job. Had Wilson hired Rita to take care of her father? Was she supposed to either marry him and persuade him to go along with the kickback, or get rid of him?

I believe I think better locked in a closet. I must remember that the next time I try to solve a mystery. She shook herself as if to check her reflexes, but then began giggling. Once she started laughing, she couldn't stop and her hysterical peals of laughter went on and on. The more she thought about the fact that she couldn't scream, but she could laugh, the funnier the situation became and the scarier.

✄✄✄

When Max arrived at the marble yard, the rain was starting to show signs of letting up. He decided not to knock on the door, fearful of alerting whoever was inside. Either Flora was with the men she had gone to confront and the scene he envi-

159

sioned was not a pleasant one, or they had already overpowered her and that was not a pleasant picture either. He cursed himself for not being at his office when the note from her had been delivered. When he got to work, his secretary, dull-witted woman that she was, had read five trivial phone messages before giving him the one from Flora. "Come to the marble yard as soon as possible. Bring help." There had been no date or time mentioned, and he wished she had seen fit to give a few other details, such as whom or what she had gone there for. The scribbling indicated how quickly she must have penned the message. Miss Sullivan had wrung her hands when questioned about the hour it had come. Finally, Max realized he was wasting time and must get over there as quickly as possible.

He stood on the left side of the building, staring into the window of a supply room, cluttered with stacks of pasteboard boxes and was startled to hear a woman's laughter; no, he corrected himself, Flora's laughter. Why would she be laughing? He shook his head confused. Then as the laughter continued, the hairs began to stand up on the back of his neck, and he realized that what sounded like hilarity was, more likely, hysteria. What was happening?

He went to the back door and tried the latch. It was locked. Was Flora there by herself? Just then he heard something bumping along the floor. The door opened a crack. He pushed his shoulder against the wood to force it open, but had no luck. The door slammed shut. "What have you done with Flora Logan?" he yelled angrily.

There was no reply. Cursing, he realized he could not cover both the front and back doors, and the men inside would escape from him unless he acted quickly. Flora's laughter ceased, a fact which he found both comforting and ominous.

He went around to the front and looked balefully up and down the street. All was quiet with no one in sight. The Boulevard was always filled with activity, buggies and wagons going to town, the trolleys going up and down the tracks, kids walking to school. But this was Saturday. He took out his pocket watch. Nine-thirty. Too late for the workers, too early for the shoppers.

He heard the hoofbeats on the brick paving before he saw who was coming. Four policemen rode furiously down the east side of the esplanade. Frantically, he ran to the broad median which was sloppy with mud from the heavy rain, waving his arms crazily in the air. Upon seeing him, they reined their horses sharply, turned left and raced the few yards across the esplanade to where he stood.

Pointing to the office of Logan's Marble Works, he bowed his head in relief and looked at the deep ruts made by the horses pawing the wet ground. He told them of the note he had received and who was in the building with Flora. "These men are probably armed; I'm afraid they'll harm Miss Logan."

The policemen nodded their heads in agreement. The leader put his finger to his lips calling for silence, and he signalled two of them to go to the exit; he and another officer moved to the entrance.

Max stood there feeling useless as he agonized about Flora's safety. He looked at her umbrella propped against the front stoop, and she came to his mind as vividly as if she were standing before him. He knew her impulsiveness had led her to do this and was sure that her actions seemed perfectly sane to her. Why had she thought it was her job to apprehend the murderers? Hadn't he shown his willingness to help? She has more personal courage than anyone I know. I don't think I've ever told her that. He wanted to do so before it was too late.

What were these men doing at Logan's anyway, and how did she find out they were going to be there? Robert Wilson was supposedly long gone. Obviously, the private investigator had made a mistake. He would bet money that Wilson was behind these doors. How many of his henchmen would he have with him? The thought of Flora being held captive by this powerful man and his friends caused Max to break out in a cold sweat. He took out his handkerchief and mopped his brow.

The morning's silence was interrupted by a policeman at the front of the building who yelled that the place was now surrounded and the occupants were to come out with their hands up.

The officers did not have to force their way into the building. Upon hearing the policeman's orders, the front door opened, and two women pranced out. Four officers and one civilian almost collapsed from shock. The men stood there stupidly shuf-

161

fling their feet in the mud. Why were these women in there? The captors gaped helplessly. In the lead was Widow Parker whose frowsy shapeless body was enclosed in a gray linen duster. Her dusty black hat quivered with dingy ostrich plumes, and she looked like a charwoman on her day off.

Rita was a different story, and as she strutted out of the building, Max remembered Flora's telling him about her father's and Caleb's attraction to this employee. The woman was dressed in love's color, a red as intense as the one who wore it. Her sateen suit was tightly fitted with a brief white lace jabot that revealed a splendid view of her ample bosom. A plump, but shapely figure, and a woman who obviously knew what to do with her curves. She wore a silly black straw hat decorated with a generous cluster of bright red cherries and topped by a bird of undetermined variety. She looked at Max and the officers and smiled, her lips glistening with something red that had been applied, her teeth gleaming whitely. The men stared appreciatively. Her sensuality was palpable and frightening. Max looked at her in confusion and realized that Flora had not yet come out.

He strode into the building and began calling her name. He stopped and listened, recognizing her voice. "Where are you?" A muffled thumping on the small door at the left of the room offered an answer to his question. The door was stuck, and he looked around for something to pry it open. With a crowbar from the supply room, he was able to unwedge the door and Flora Logan tumbled out.

Red-faced and breathless, she gasped, "Where are they?"

"Who, Wilson? He's gone, but the women are still here." Max explained.

"That's who I mean, Rita and Mrs. Parker."

He took her to the front door, and when she realized the women were with four policemen, she gave a sigh and collapsed in a chair. "Rita killed Ward Fain and my father. She's a murderess, and Bertie Parker's her accomplice."

Her revelation shocked Max who looked at her as if she'd lost her senses. Hastily, he stepped to the front door, noticing the fifth officer who had arrived in a wagon. He watched for a moment as the woman in red began to take control. Max went

162

up to the officer who had just come and was ogling Rita as he struggled to maintain his composure.

"I'm Officer Ryan and I need to ask you some questions, Miss Campbell. You remember I met you at the boarding house when your friend . . ." The policeman's voice was hardly more than a croak.

"Of course, Officer Ryan."

"Did the men who Miss Logan suspects get away?

Rita smiled and answered, "Yes sir, they left right before you came. Said they were catching the noon train to St. Louis." She looked at Widow Parker who nodded in agreement.

Officer Ryan wrote this information on the tablet he hastily pulled from his coat pocket. "How come you ladies are here?"

"We're just leaving, Officer . . ." Rita sidled toward the street.

Max stepped in front of her and informed Ryan that the women were criminals and must be taken into custody and jailed. Ryan looked from Rita to Max, hesitated briefly, then apologized to Rita as he braceleted her wrists.

When Max came back, he looked at Flora worriedly. She was babbling incoherently. He knelt beside her in order to hold her hands and stroked her long tapered fingers and delicate wrists. He smoothed her tangled hair gently until she breathed normally.

"I didn't think you'd ever come. My note was stupid, but I didn't know what to say. Until I got here and talked to Rita, I wasn't positive she was the murderer." She filled him in briefly on the confession which Rita made and the clothing she had found in the cloak closet.

"I understand. Don't worry about it. You are incredibly clever. How did you figure it all out? I hadn't any idea who the killer was."

"Once I remembered where I'd seen the belladonna growing, it all fell into place." She told him of her trip to the library and the cards with Rita's name on them. "I couldn't go to the police with evidence of a suspect's name on a library card. I had to confront her and hope she'd admit what she'd done. And, thankfully, she did."

"I feel so stupid. I was certain Robert Wilson was in there with you, and I wanted to break his neck and maybe yours, too." Max stood and patted her head. "I think you were very brave, a little foolhardy, perhaps, but very courageous. I know the police are going to be grateful for the help you've given them; they may not tell you this, but I know that they'll feel a lot of gratitude."

"Is Sergeant Ryan out there?"

"I don't know, what does he look like?"

"Like a large bouncing ball."

"Yes, he's definitely there. He just arrived. He wasn't part of the mounted police officers who came first."

"No, I would not think horseback riding is a possibility for him." She laughed and that reminded Max of what he had heard.

"Flora, why were you laughing earlier? That's what I heard when I walked up to the building."

"Good, I'm glad I accomplished something. I was laughing because I couldn't scream. Rita and Mrs. Parker mocked me for being too scared to yell."

"You know, I was scared too. It is difficult for me to accept that I'm in love with a woman who always does the unexpected. I don't want to change you, but I would like to protect you from danger. I don't know how."

Flora blushed and pinched the fabric of her skirt between her thumb and middle finger. Max waited for her to speak. She said nothing.

"Flora, did you hear what I said. I'm bound over to you, and it frightens me because in the two months I've known you, I've seen you plunge headlong into all kinds of dangers with no thoughts of your own well-being. And things have been said that make me think I don't know all the trouble you've been involved in."

"You are right; you don't."

"Well, should I know everything? Should I just stand by for the rest of my life watching you jump from one frightening adventure into another?"

"Yes, I guess so. I mean, that's what I wish you would do. Because I want you to be there for me. That is what I desire above all else."

"Is this your way of saying that you care for me? I'm afraid I need something more than a hint." Max spoke more forcefully than he intended.

"Yes, I do, Max, and I think I always shall." Flora looked up at him. Max slowly stood, drew her to her feet, and looked deeply into her splendid, laughing eyes. So lost were they in their new-found feelings, they failed to realize that Sergeant Ryan had entered the office.

"'Scuse me, Miss Logan, but I need to ask a few questions. Are you Miss Logan's attorney, Mr. Andrews? She threatened to call you a couple of days ago. That was when we suspected her of murdering Mr. Fain."

Max looked questioningly at Flora; she studied the wooden floorboards. "Yes, I am and, as such, I am asking for your questions to be brief. She's been through a lot."

"She looks fine to me, Sir. I don't think much fazes this lady. She's real spunky! To think of her taking on these two criminals by herself, unarmed and defenseless; it's really incredible, isn't it? The newshounds are gonna have a field day with this one, aren't they?"

"Yes, I'm afraid you're right about the journalists. I agree with you completely regarding her spunkiness, Officer, and by the way, she looks fine to me too."

It had been a day of surprises for Flora, but when Max brought her home, another one awaited her, a letter from Aunt Ruth. As soon as she was in her room, she slipped the envelope from her pocket and slit it open.

My dearest Flora,

I received your letter and with mixed feelings will reveal the secret which I have been party to for twenty-two years. Your mother was my dearest friend and was engaged to my older brother Sam. They were so in love and when he died of Typhoid, she wanted to die as well. She came to me and revealed she was with child. My thoughts were for her not to bear a baby out of wedlock and for my dead brother, so his child would have a father. I told my parents, and together we convinced my younger brother Fred to marry your mother. He

165

acted willing to do so and completely understood the situation.

At the time, it seemed the best solution, and I still feel it was preferable to the other options. But I understood how difficult this marriage was for everyone, especially when he made you leave home. I question if he would have done that had he been your birth father.

When you received the telegram announcing your father's death, I wanted to tell you the truth, but held back for fear you wouldn't return to Texas if you had known he wasn't your real father. You needed to go back there and confront the ghosts of your past. I hope you can forgive me for meddling in your life all these years.

Love,
Aunt Ruth

Flora was glad she was sitting down, for she thought she would have fallen otherwise. She felt sad for her parents who had lived in a loveless marriage, and she felt sad for herself, having never known a father's love, but she also felt free. The past was behind her, and she no longer would feel bitter about not measuring up to her father's expectations. The burden of his censure was gone. She was glad she had learned the truth. What if Aunt Ruth had died without telling her?

When she realized all that had happened in the last two months, she had to wonder where her life was going. The unmasking of Rita Campbell, the excitement of a new career in Houston, the opening of her heart to a man who had proved he would treat it carefully, and now the revelation about her father. Any one of these would have been enough. As she lay down to take a nap, her last thoughts were that God was truly watching over her.

CHAPTER SIXTEEN

The two-story Queen Anne home at 1011 Heights Boulevard had been the scene of unprecedented flurry for the past forty-eight hours. Dessie and Flora had almost lived there as they readied everything for the wedding, Dessie fretting over the cost of the wedding flowers, and Flora not pointing out that was why most brides married in June instead of November. But they were able to get roses for the bouquets and the altar and had used a simple green and white color scheme for the dining room. After all, Flora thought wryly, one can only do so much with chrysanthemums. She had arranged a large bouquet of the gold and lavender blossoms in a tall wrought iron floor vase of Mrs. Webber's, placing it in the front hall next to the table with the guest book. By trailing long stems of English ivy down to the floor and filling in the holes with asparagus fern, she felt that it was presentable.

Samuel Webber, a successful brick mason had built his two story red brick home four years before. He and Carter Standley were first business associates and then had become close friends despite their age difference. When Carter became engaged to Dessie, Mr. Webber and his wife took the couple under their wing and offered to host the wedding ceremony and reception in their home.

The handsome white brick fireplace with its unique red brick circular supports designed by Sam Webber had become an improvised altar covered with palm branches, pink roses and white carnations intertwined with smilax. The varnished cypress sliding doors opened to a formal dining room where the wedding table was covered with white tulle and satin. Narrow streamers attached to the chandelier trailed down, gracefully bisecting the table. Large silver trays waited at each end of the table to be filled with the spicy meat pies and boiled shrimps. The silver bride's basket was filled with chocolate bonbons and the tiered wedding cake was the focal point of the entire room. Mrs. Webber had insisted they use her cut glass vases now filled with white carnations, candytuft, and feathery ferns and placed at each end of the lace runner covering the buffet. The girls stood back to admire the results.

167

"Anything would look gorgeous in these vases."

"Oh, Flora, everyone seems so happy for Carter and me. Don't you think it's because we live in a small community? I don't think people in Houston are this close."

Flora was able to agree with Dessie more good-naturedly now than she would have two weeks ago. A short time had passed but much had occurred, not the least of which was the ease she felt around people here in the Heights. Her aggressiveness in solving the murder of Ward Fain seemed to have brought about the community's acceptance of her actions as productive and commendable, rather than crazy and eccentric. As a young girl, she had sometimes felt isolated from the townspeople, someone who did not belong or fit in. Now, she felt at home, and she had decided she would not return to New York City. Not because of Max Andrews, though he was a part of her decision, but because her roots here would enable her to live a worthwhile and productive life.

"Don't the streamers look elegant, Flora?"

"Yes, everything is perfect. Now let's go upstairs and make you into a bride. You have dirt on your nose and leaves in your hair, and in just three hours, the guests will arrive." She giggled at Dessie's kid rollers which were starting to fall out, spilling golden curls all down her shoulders. The two women embraced spontaneously. "I won't be able to give you a wedding day hug once we are in our finery."

The girls made their way up the three-level staircase, anchored by square carved cypress posts which had been polished until the rich wood gleamed. Mr. and Mrs. Webber had insisted they dress in the master bedroom, and when the girls saw their dresses spread out on the large four poster bed, they gasped with excitement.

After taking their baths in the porcelain claw-footed tub, they began the hour and half job of pinning up their hair. Finally, they were ready to dress. Flora slipped into the pink taffeta under-dress and put on a deep rose chiffon fingertip tunic banded with crystal bead fringe. She took out her mother's jewelry box and chose a brooch with loops of tiny seed pearls, which she pinned in the center of her bodice. Then she put on the pearl drop earrings, tilting her head so that they grazed her cheeks.

Stepping to the curved alcove, she pushed aside the lace curtain and looked out the oriole window to the Boulevard below. The late afternoon sun lengthened the shadows across the lawn. Spindly watermelon red crape myrtles, planted inside the iron railing which bordered the corner lot, still had a few blooms. She saw the Logan buggy pull up in front of the house. Caleb, tall and gangly in his new dark blue suit hopped out and tied Lucy's reins to one of the square concrete posts that flanked the front sidewalk. Then he hurried around to help his companion alight. Julia Brown stepped out of the carriage, paused and adjusted her skirt. Flora craned her neck to see what she wore. "Oh, Dessie, here's Caleb and Julia. I can hardly wait to see her dress. " She watched as Caleb then helped Mrs. Brown down. "The organist is here now."

"Come help me, I'm about to tear something." Dessie cried out.

Mrs. Webber came in at that moment and lifted the chantilly lace bodice which had caught on the petticoat hook. She held the dress open while Dessie stepped in and fastened the tiny covered buttons which extended down the back from the high satin collarband to her hips. Layers of white silk chiffon billowed around her ankles.

"Who did you say sewed this dress?" Mrs. Webber asked, pushing up her spectacles and examining the seams in the lace.

"Mrs. Duffy. Why?" Dessie asked holding her breath, knowing what an accomplished seamstress Jenny Webber was.

"I couldn't have done better myself!" she exclaimed as she spread the lace tunic over the chiffon. "You look lovely."

"You're a beautiful bride!" Flora chimed in.

"All brides are beautiful, and you're just saying that because you're my best friend. Look how pretty you are in your rose-colored chiffon. It's pretty daring to dress a redhead in pink, but you look wonderful."

Flora was pleased. She turned to hide her blush and studied the green tiled hearth in front of the polished mahogany mantel, looking down at the top of her high-heeled ivory kid pumps. Turning back to face Dessie, she put one foot behind and gave a mock curtsy as a thank-you for the compliment.

169

Mrs. Webber lifted the tulle veil attached to a short em-broidered headband, and placed it toward the front of Dessie's hair. The short train billowed out over her shoulders and all three women felt tears in their eyes. "I wish your mother were here to see you, Dessie," Mrs. Webber said.

"She died when I was a baby, so I never knew her. It's hard to miss what you've never known. Aunt Ferdie is here, and she's the mother I've loved all these years. She has love for me and her newsboy orphans, and more to spare."

"What do I have more of to spare?" Aunt Ferdie asked as she entered the room carrying the bouquets. She stopped stock still when she saw her niece as a bride. "Oh, you are a beautiful bride." They laughed at her words, Ferdie looking at them in confusion.

"That's just what Flora said," Dessie explained.

The girls ran to take the flowers she held. Dessie's bou-quet was a massive arrangement of bridal white roses. Flora oohed and ahhed. "It's a large bouquet for such a petite bride. There must be, yes, there are two dozen roses and look at the lily-of-the-valley. Isn't it dear. Whom did Carter say did the ar-rangement?"

"Kutschbach's does everything for him. Carter always buys a vase of fresh flowers and puts it in the front hall of each home he finishes building."

"Well, it's a nice idea, and he's a wonderful man that you're getting ready to marry." Aunt Ferdie smiled and Dessie beamed with happiness.

"It's the prettiest bridal bouquet I've ever seen." Jennie Webber declared.

Flora picked up her nosegay of pink and white roses nestled in a bed of maidenhair fern and baby's breath, the long white satin ribbons tied in love knots at the ends. "I hear the organ music downstairs. Julia's mother is warming up."

"Do you have your penny in your shoe?"

"Yes, of course. I hope it doesn't make my toe cramp."

A knock on the bedroom door was followed by a voice re-minding them the time had come. Nervously, Dessie drew on her short lace mitts, and went to the threshhold looking up at Judge Milroy with a serious and unwavering expression. She announced she was ready, and the judge beamed, mopped his face, stuffed his handkerchief into his pocket, and held out his arm. They stepped back allowing Flora to precede them.

Her head held high, the maid of honor floated down the beautiful stairway, pausing at the first landing to make sure the guests realized the wedding had begun. Standing just to the left at the foot of the stairs, were Max Andrews and Jesse Jones. She drew a quick breath, blushed the color of her dress, smiled, and slowly passed them.

Flora would always remember the picture of Dessie coming down the stairway to the strains of Lohengrin's wedding music played by Mrs. Brown, the ooh's and aah's of the guests, and the look on the couple's faces when Mr. Brown pronounced them man and wife. Dessie's hopefulness and optimism which rose from the depths of her soul had long been a source of strength for Flora, and she was glad to be here for her friend, to share this important day with her and to bask in the warm feelings of the people who had gathered.

The ceremony drew to a close with the bridal couple exchanging a brief kiss. In seconds Max was at her side and Mr. Jones as well. They extended compliments on the bride's loveliness, but all the while, Max gazed at Flora in a way that left no doubt as to whom he thought was loveliest. Flora held the nosegay up to her face and sniffed the roses to hide her confusion. She wondered if her time had come now that the bizarre happenings of the past two months had ended. Her ill-fated trip to the Big Thicket had stretched forward, leaping over the last four years and setting in motion a string of events which forever shaped her life. She felt confident the murder of Fred Logan was not planned by Ward Fain and thus had not stemmed from anything she had done. This knowledge had relieved her. She grieved for the violent death of the man she had thought was her father, but realized his gullibility and male vanity had caused the murder, not any action of hers.

"The police haven't located Robert Wilson, I'm sorry to say." Jesse Jones interrupted her thoughts, though his subject matter paralleled hers. Flora guessed she would always wonder if Rita acted out of anger at being spurned or had taken directions from the foreman who may have wanted to eliminate her father. The woman had steadfastly refused to implicate Robert Wilson, and that's the way the case would go to trial.

"I imagine he's long gone. He's probably in California by now; there's a building boom in San Francisco. I hate to admit it, but he'll get another job as a foreman working for someone who's impressed by his abilities and doesn't see the man's depravity. I'm sorry I misjudged him so completely." Jones shook his head ruefully. "If I hadn't, this job would have had a different ending."

Flora and Max looked at each other solemnly, knowing that while they both preferred that the tragedies not have occurred, it was doubtful Flora would have returned to the Heights had her father not been killed. Max joked once that she would have remained in his memory as the redhead who had worn a gold satin banner. Robert Wilson and his manipulation of the people involved in the building of the Rice Hotel had dramatically altered their lives.

"You know, I don't build these buildings for the rent check I get from them. Money loaned and interest compounded would bring a better financial return than investments in buildings without the vexations and hazards." Jesse Jones spoke, and several men formed a circle around him to listen. "But I find no fun in lending money, and there is a great deal of fun and satisfaction in planning and building. This is what makes me the happiest." Several of the men clapped. "I am grieved about what happened at the Rice Hotel. The safe and sound construction of my buildings has always been my first and foremost goal. I have learned from this experience, however, and I pledge to be evermindful of the lengths to which men will go to get their hands on the almighty dollar. It's a lesson I won't forget." He looked at Flora though he had already privately extended his apologies. "This young lady has agreed to remain in Houston and take over the management of the company her father began. She and her cousin will now run Logan & Logan Marble Works." Another smattering of applause rippled through the group, and Max squeezed Flora's elbow in approval.

Many cups of punch were drunk that evening, and many toasts were given to the bridal couple, but Flora would always remember best the toast which was extended to her by Judge

Milroy. "Miss Logan, the Heights is grateful for your courage and your intelligence which enabled you to see that which escaped the rest of us. We are delighted that you are once more with us, and we hope you stay here always." Everyone in the room clapped loudly, and Flora looked from face to face, realizing that she intended to do just that.

HISTORICAL NOTES

Houston Heights

A planned suburban streetcar community which got its name because its elevation is twenty-three feet higher than downtown Houston, Texas. Developers began selling lots in 1892, and the city became incorporated in 1896, with its own mayor, marshall, tax collector, water company, and fire department. It grew to a population of about 8,000 and was incorporated into the city of Houston in 1918.

The community today is a thriving historical district with a unique small-town flavor and commitment to preservation.

Jesse Holman Jones (1874-1956)

Jones was a major builder in Houston, Texas, where he put up a total of fifty buildings. His settling here was a windfall for Houston. Without his wise leadership, public service, and philanthropy, this city would not occupy the position it does.

Hortense Sparks Ward (1892-1944)

Mrs. Ward was a resident of Houston Heights for several years while she studied law by correspondence. The first woman in Texas to pass the bar examination, she practiced law until 1939, but never appeared in court on a client's behalf because to do so would have prejudiced the jury against her case. She was the first woman in line to register to vote following the ratification of the nineteenth amendment. In 1925 when the Texas supreme court justices had to disqualify themselves from hearing a case, the governor appointed her to serve as chief justice.

Ferdie Trichelle (c1870-?)

A resident of Houston Heights, Miss Trichelle organized the Emma R. Newsboys Home, which she named for her mother.

Elizabeth Britton (1858-1934)

A botanist, who is credited for suggesting New York City should have a great botanical garden, she was married to Nathaniel Britton, first director-in-chief of the New York Botanical Gardens. In addition to her work with mosses, Elizabeth Britton was the chief proponent and founder of the Wild Flower Preservation Society of America in April, 1902, and was elected its secretary and treasurer. She authored 346 scientific papers.

O. M. Carter (1842-1928)

Native of Massachusetts, he came to Texas after a career which ranged from tinner to Indian agent to bank president. He bought 1765 acres northwest of Houston, Texas where he and his associates developed a planned suburban community. He is considered the founder of Houston Heights.

Annette Finnigan (1871-1940)

A Wellesley graduate, Miss Finnigan handled her father's considerable business interests after his death, serving as president of the Brazos Hotel. She was probably responsible for its reputation as a safe place for women travellers to stay. In 1903 she organized Houston's Equal Suffrage Association and was elected president.

The Big Thicket

A national preserve, 95,316 acres in Southeast Texas, consisting of ten different ecosystems and a biological diversity that ranges from fifty kinds of reptiles to thirty varieties of wild orchids.

REFERENCES

Agatha, Sister M., *The History of Houston Heights, 1891-1918*. Houston: Premier Printing Company, 1956.

Brown, Henry Justus. *The Sermons, 1910-1918*. Unpublished collection. St. Andrew's Episcopal Church Library.

Edey, Maitland A. *This Fabulous Century: Sixty Years of American Life*, Vol. I and II. New York: Time Life Books, 1969.

Foxworth, Erna B. *The Romance of Old Sylvan Beach: A Hundred Years of Amusement and Nostalgia.* Austin: Waterway Press, 1986.

Good Housekeeping Magazine. Volume LII, 1911. New York: The Phelps Publishing Company.

Houghton, Dorothy Knox Howe, et. al. *Houston's Forgotten Heritage, Landscape, Houses, Interiors, 1824-1914.* Houston: Rice University Press, 1991.

The Houson Chronicle

The Houston Daily Post

The Houston Press

Howard, Dorothy. *Dorothy's World, Childhood in Sabine Bottom, 1902-1910*. Englewood Cliffs, New Jersey: Prentice-Hall, Inc., 1977.

Johnston, Marguerite. *Houston, The Unknown City, 1836-1946.* College Station: Texas A&M University Press, 1991.

    This Happy Worldly Abode, Christ Church Cathedral 1839-1964. Houston: Cathedral Press, 1964.

Lincoln, Mrs. Mary J., et al. *Home Helps, A Pure Food Cookbook.* New York: The N. K. Fairbank Company, 1910.

Love, Mrs. W.G., editor, *The Key to the City of Houston,* December 1908.

Pace, G.Randle and Deborah Markey. *Houston Heights, 1891-1991, A Historical Portrait and Comtemporary Perspective.* Houston: Tribune Publishing Company, 1991.

Peacock, Howard. *The Big Thicket of Texas, America's Ecological Wonder.* Boston: Little, Brown & Company, 1984.

Robinson, Robert E. and Martha N. Robinson. *Dr. Robinson, His Life and Times.* Privately published, 1993.

Rothman, Sheila M. *Woman's Proper Place, A History of Changing Ideals and Practices, 1870 to the Present. New York: Basic Books, Inc., 1978.*

Sanders, Jack. *Hedgemaids and Fairy Candles, The Lives and Lore of North American Wildflowers.* Camden, Me: Ragged Mountain Press, 1993.

Stougaard, M. H. *Life of William Frederick Thurow, Botanist of Texas.* Unpublished Manuscript in Peabody Library Special Collection, Sam Houston University.

The Suburbanite, Heights Newspaper, January, 1905-February, 1920.

Timmons, Bascom N. *Jesse H. Jones, The Man and the Statesman.* New York: Henry Holt and Company, 1956.

Ward, Mrs. Hortense, "Shall Women Have Adequate Laws?" *The Texas Magazine*, Volume IV, January 1913, pp 239-242.

Wilson, Ann Quin. *Native Houstonian.* Norfolk: Houston Baptist University Press, 1982.

✄✄✄